SINCE THIS BOO[K]

OTHER TITLES EX[IST]

AUTHOR :— 'PILLARS OF FIRE'

WHEN THE MOON CAME

AROUT TO BE PUBLISHED :—

'CULTURAL SHOCK'

PENDING :——

'THE HUMAN ENIGMA'

'THE SECOND COMING'

'REALLY ??'

Monkey Trial 2000

L. Mason Jones served a number of years in the military, and travelling on a so-called 'government service' passport, found himself in such places as south Yemen, Bahrain, the Gulf of Oman, Cyprus and Germany. After leaving the service he became part of the team producing the highly successful business jet, The Hawker 125. He functioned as a quality engineering inspector with, initially, British Aerospace then Corporate Jets Inc and finally Raytheon USA, the latter of which purchased the thriving business and moved production to the USA. Mr Jones then left the business to concentrate on writing projects. He has three adult offspring and resides in Chester.

Monkey Trial 2000

2000

L. Mason Jones

Arena Books

First published in 2019 by Arena Books

Arena Books
6 Southgate Green
Bury St. Edmunds
IP33 2BL

www.arenabooks.co.uk

Distributed in America by Ingram International, One Ingram Blvd., P.O. Box
3006, La Vergne, TN 37086-1985, USA.

L. Mason Jones

Monkey Trial 2000

British Library cataloguing in Publication Data. A Catalogue record
for this book is available from the British Library.

ISBN-13   978-1-911593-39-3

BIC classifications:- FA, FHP, FMR, FQ.

Printed and bound by Lightning Source UK

Cover design
By Jason Anscomb

Typeset in
Times New Roman

INTRODUCTION

This is the story of John Willoughby, an anthropologist of the new millennium. His recently published book *The Human Enigma* was rapidly becoming a bestseller and had provoked intense controversy between the theologians and scientists not hitherto seen for over three generations. A few of his contemporaries distanced themselves from his work and viewed him as a radical or non-conformist. John realised that he had opened up an old wound and again raised the spectre that had long haunted the profession, regarding the continually elusive vital fossil links that still remain undiscovered, in order to finally solve the mystery of human origins. John had exposed the unresolved issues and made it clear that no theory for human origins could be viewed as unassailable or written in stone. An eminent member of his profession had stated "no one can stand up and declare that they know how it happened." John felt that this statement could apply to any belief system for how humans 'came to be' and make it clear that other alternatives were still open to anyone setting out to explore the question of human beings. To make his point he introduced a wealth of circumstantial evidence that was alleged to support a fantastic 'third alternative' to explain the amazing human brain and intellect, which at its best separates' humans by light years from any alleged simian ancestor. Now, the frequent and fiery debates throughout the media were not simply between the so-called 'creationists' and 'evolutionists', astronomers, astrophysicists and even ufologists joined their number. The press reviews of John's book asked, "What do we believe?" and "Are humans ET hybrids?" and called it *Darwin Revisited*. John Willoughby was a person who would shun publicity rather than court it, but now he found himself attending a series of one to one TV and radio interviews that took up most of his week. But, he could not afford to anguish over all the controversy and publicity engendered by publication of his book, simply because to promote widespread discussion was precisely the reason he had written it.

John Willoughby entered his study, poured himself a drink then slumped into his favourite chair. He rubbed his chin and began to contemplate the hectic events of the recent past. "How did it all happen?" he thought, then paused momentarily. A wry smile crossed his lips as he considered the poignancy for this self questioning remark. "Indeed, how did it happen?" His long contemplation and analysis of that question was the subject of his recently published book and the after effects, which included all the recent disruption in his life and the voluminous deluge of mail that he had received after publication of *The Human Enigma*.

Some of his correspondence could only be described as hate mail. However, along with these rather disturbing tirades which he felt judged him harshly and unfairly; he also received an abundance of the comforting and encouraging kind. As a result, it had become clear to him that many other people shared his view, that widespread debate on an open forum regarding such an important issue had been long overdue. They pointed out and concurred that rarely, if ever, had the issues and anomalies he had raised been openly admitted or at least discussed on prime-time television and radio programmes. Now of course, the opposite was the case.

On the positive side, John and his family now enjoyed, largely due to the proceeds from his book, a much-improved lifestyle and experienced the benefits of his new-found success. Here he was, suddenly transformed from a person that nobody in the literary world had even heard of, to someone who had become almost a household name. He has been thrust into a limelight of controversy and a constant round of radio and television appearances. He had only agreed to such appearances if they were to be on a 'one to one' basis for the simple reason that all the data, facts, evidence, anomalies and shortcomings of the various theories presented in his book were well known even if not widely discussed by others before him and were not his own radical assumptions and notions. Therefore, having nothing to defend, he refused to put himself 'in the dock' as he described it, by appearing alone to face a panel of academic, scholarly inquisitors attempting to make the heretic recant. And in any case, he did not like the media attention, and although he felt obliged to attend these one-to-one appointments for his agent, his publishers and indeed his own benefit with regard to the promotion and subsequent sales of his book, he hated them enormously. In the first place he was a very private person, and in his own view he did not feel that he was at all photogenic and was not fond of the sound of his own voice. Nevertheless, he tolerated it all for cold commercial reasons and his family's wellbeing but disliked it intensely.

Now, there was this coming TV show called 'How did it happen?' that dealt with mysterious and controversial issues. It was already completed and 'in the can' and would be shown this evening on a prime-time TV slot.

John's thoughts ranged back to a few years ago, when apart from the routine problems that everyone's family experiences, peace and tranquillity reigned for the most part in his life as he got on with his work, it was then that he had begun his final manuscript. Strangely, he had originally titled it 'How did it happen? 'But changed the title to The *Human Enigma* before the TV programme was even thought of. If he had possessed the clairvoyance to know what would ultimately happen, no doubt he would have quickly changed it back again. In any case, at the time he had felt that, quite probably, none of the usual publishing houses that dealt with the more academic works relative to his own profession would dare to handle his rather controversial book. *The Human Enigma* was the result of well over a decade of interest and research into the anomalies and mysteries existing not only in the theory pertaining to the Darwinian viewpoint, but the whole concept of Genesis and divine human creation, through to the more radical and fantastic proposition of this so-called 'third alternative'. John's aim was to remain detached and to present the facts and data and highlight the mysteries in an impartial manner, but the subject of the third alternative after a full analysis of it began to become strangely compelling and it disturbed his preferred impartiality. This was simply because an abundance of circumstantial evidence emerged that appeared to support it.

CONTENTS

CHAPTER I

HOW DID IT HAPPEN?

John Willoughby felt very fortunate that he had made a friend in the form of David Villiers, who turned out to be a very useful contact indeed. David was a barrister a politician and a TV personality, as well as being related by marriage to a publisher, whose organisation was not averse to material of a controversial nature. Were it not for these simple facts, he felt that he would still be facing an uphill struggle to find a publisher willing to handle an academic challenge. David's connections with the world of television were an obvious advantage, and it was David who would present the programme based on John's book that he and his family would view tonight.

When he had first begun to write *The Human Enigma*, he had considered that it might not be sufficiently voluminous to offer for publication, but after an in-depth analysis of the amazing proposition that he chose to call 'the third alternative', he had begun to realise that enough material seemed to exist for a complete and separate chapter on its own. As a result, he was able to complete *The Human Enigma* in three distinct sections which would, in addition to highlighting the obvious lack of discussion and widespread debate, that in his view ought to be occurring on an open forum, also fully analyse each of the primary belief systems regarding the subject that he felt was the most important issue of our time. With the rapid advancement of human technology and discovery, together with the compelling urge to travel into the cosmos, it seemed clear that humans knew where they were ultimately going yet seemed unable to explain where they came from.

Now after publication of his work John felt reasonably confident that he had achieved his aim, of making people aware that no theory for human origins could simply be dismissed or written off, as long as any evidence existed, even if it was purely circumstantial, that could be shown to support it, and that other alternatives were still open to us. It had long been clear to John that the Darwinian theory, although being the most scientifically acceptable, had many important questions to address, particularly in the later stages of human emergence, where the amazing and rapid development of the human brain and its intelligence capacity streaked light years ahead of any alleged primate 'relative'. As for the third alternative and its rather amazing proposition, the substantial amount of circumstantial evidence that John had encountered that appeared to support it and that had been offered and subscribed to by various writers, and even a few academics ever since the late Charles Fort suggested human kind might be property, had intrigued him greatly. John however, chose an open-minded approach. But, the reason for his developing interest in this fantastic proposition, that many of the unexplained oddities regarding the theories and assumptions subscribed to for human origins, all appeared to fall neatly into place and therefore stimulated his further interest. It was largely for these reasons that he felt it virtually qualified itself for inclusion in his work, as an alternative belief system. Although trained, experienced and well versed in his chosen profession and being, as he put it 'compelled but not yet convinced' regarding the assumption of primate ancestry, he knew that many vital questions still remained unaddressed. Particularly, in regard to the last 50 thousand years in the process of human emergence, which he liked to describe as 'supernatural' evolution rather than a natural process. John found himself mentally sympathising with Charles Darwin's contemporary Alfred Russell Wallace, who in his failure to identify or quantify the unknown variable or exterior force responsible for the unique human qualities, diverted from it completely. John was aware that when Darwin wrote 'Origins' not a single ancient fossil had been found, it was entirely theory. And, that a British scientist had highlighted around 800 phrases in the subjunctive mood in his work such as 'let us assume' and 'we may well suppose' and so forth. He also knew that the late Sir Arthur Keith, the eminent medical anthropologist, had studied the genetic traits of apes and humans and found 312 distinct features only applicable to the human, compared to 109 in the chimpanzee and 75 in the gorilla. Arthur Keith had stated "whatever theory is propounded, it would have to account for these major functional differences."

Many of these unique human traits were simply ignored or taken for granted by many in his profession, who saw the human as little more than a naked ape.

Why was the human naked anyway, after a process that amply provided other creatures with adequate protection, yet failed completely to protect the dominant species? Surely, this made the human appear to be unrelated to earthly evolution at all.

It was not acceptable to John Willoughby to be told that dwelling on genetic traits or unique human gifts was simply a form of self-aggrandisement. To be sure, basic creativity was evident in certain other creatures such as birds when building their nests, beavers with their dams and bees with their precise honeycombs. But such creativity was all relative to an earthly environment. Apes were distinctively uncreative, but human creativity was immense and profound, and the gifts of imagination, pre-planning and envisaging scenarios before creating them, the capacity for mathematics and the greatly developed and over-endowed brain, could not be dismissed by accusations of mere self-aggrandisement. Although John could not condone a blinkered and slavish adherence to the mainstream view of his profession without any serious attempt to analyse the pitfalls and anomalies, he could quite understand it. John had been brought up in the Catholic faith and even though diverting from its rigid doctrines, remained respectful of it, and he wished that he could accept every word of Genesis as true. However, it was clear that anyone living 140 years ago, who had rejected former beliefs in favour of the 'new messiah' as Charles Darwin could be called, really had nowhere else to turn if simian ancestry remained unproven. Unless they chose to embrace the so-called 'third alternative' he had offered for consideration in *The Human Enigma*. He felt that with regard to his contemporaries, there would be little chance of that possibility arising, on the contrary, they would dismiss it out of hand and would regard even the acknowledgement of it as a form of professional suicide. During his own observations, John had found many anomalies in the scrappy human fossil record and its disjointed and perplexing discoveries such as very ancient skull fragments, subsequently to be called 'Swanscombe Man', appearing to be more anatomically modern than the more pithecoid Neanderthals who appeared much later. And certainly, the six or seven hominid skull fossils appear to be unrelated. Swanscombe man was deduced from just a few small portions and the fragmented hominid skulls, all seemed so 'pithecoid' in spite of their dentition and so forth, and Neanderthal was totally unrelated to the only convincing ancestors, the Cro-Magnon-aurignation people from whom all current humanity descends. Although genetic change within kind had occurred in the horse for example, which was once the size of a large dog, any species change from one creature to another was a different matter. Yet, the whole process from lungfish to human demanded the occurrence of many such changes of species. When he was researching his material for the third alternative, John had encountered an interesting suggestion regarding the horse, which was, that the same genetic engineering process occurred concerning the horse, that formed the third alternative; in order for it to be suitably equipped to assist the developing human so ably in his farming and transportation requirements. He regarded this proposition as at least food for thought if nothing else.

John had given up any attempts to discuss the anomalies that he felt bedevilled the Darwinian theory with his colleagues, as on the few occasions he had done so, he had always felt like someone trying to convince the Pope that there was no God. And so, his poor wife Carol, found herself on the receiving end of his frustrated laments. Although she politely feigned interest, he knew the subject simply wasn't her bag. But John was no less guilty in his reaction to some of the topics she enthusiastically related to him, relative to her own interests. In his profession, John had never felt comfortable, using, or indeed hearing such expressions as our 'cousins' the chimpanzees or our 'ancestors' the primates, until it was clear that they could place the final and compelling bones or skeletons on the fossil table. He couldn't blame those who used such expressions, as they were only following the example set by their mentor Charles Darwin; who boldly stated that gorillas and chimpanzees were man's closest living relatives, when not a single ancient fossil had been found. John felt that his profession had acted like a fast-talking salesman pushing a contract in front of the layman and stating "don't worry it's all been sorted, trust me, sign here please" with a palm firmly covering the small print which read; fully proven subject to the finding of the conclusive bone fossil evidence.

With regard to the first and second parts of his book, anything John had written about, or highlighted, could be studied by anyone who wished to take the trouble to access the reference books and works freely available in any good library, that dealt with the current human bone fossil evidence and the latest paleo-anthropological discoveries. The same approach could also be utilized to study the many theological works and biblical texts. In particular, the Old Testament and the writings of Genesis relating to the beliefs in biblical human creation.

When John first began to write his manuscript, the first section began with a close study of the theory of interest to his own profession, and the data and evidence, or more specifically the lack of it regarding our assumed primate ancestry as per the thoughts of Charles Darwin. John had long been aware that a certain pre-conceived notion seemed to exist with regard to the subject of dry dusty bones and those active in the field who studied them. The View seemed to be in place that paleo-anthropological data was pursued and compiled by gentlemen in late middle age who smoked pipes and wore tweedy jackets with leather patches on the elbows. John himself failed to meet this description on most counts. However, the general feeling the public seemed to maintain was that the subject in any case was all wrapped up by the academics and scholars, and that with regard to human origins of the Darwinian kind, all the facts were in. Whereas, it was possible that some of those in his profession might be happy to condone this false assumption, John knew, and was well aware that most of his colleagues knew, that this was simply not the case. It was clear to John, that many people whose strong religious views precluded it in any case, had neither the inclination, nor took the time to review the data currently available for themselves. In any case, he thought, even those who are unsure, or neutral regarding the issue generally, for the most part put their trust in science to come up with all the answers, while they themselves simply get on with their own professions. Such people were quite vulnerable to auto-suggestion and as John was well aware how many of them had been continually subjected to a barrage of constant references to primate ancestors and chimpanzee cousins, which, of course they may very well be, it was natural to conclude that many of them would assume that all the facts were in. John knew, that the entire Darwinian package, as it had been described, had slowly but surely, and undoubtedly assisted by such remarks, taken on an image of unquestionable truth, and had gradually transformed itself from a theory into a widely accepted dogma over the decades, without any proportional increase in compelling bone fossil evidence at all. And was now deemed to be quite unassailable. John Willoughby, through his book, wanted to reach these people who were convinced this was so without reviewing the evidence for themselves, and introduce them to the idea, that," although the theory may be perfectly true, it had not been conclusively proven to be so, and that other alternatives still remained open to them.

He was aware of course, that it was this attitude that had brought about his reputation as a radical or non-conformist, even a traitor within his profession. He was quite aware that he had not endeared himself to his colleagues with his views, and that even before the publication of *The Human Enigma* he was regarded as a maverick or a pariah within their profession.

It had always perplexed him how some of his colleagues could be so blasé and casual about the process that John liked to call supernatural evolution. A process that occurred in mere thousands of years from the Homo-erectus entity, who bowed out some 500 thousand years ago and who still had the skull of an ape; up to the emergence of the Cro-Magnon types commonly known as the Aurignation peoples. They had appeared suddenly, mysteriously and with no predecessor, upright, anatomically modern, artistic and creatively intelligent and are the only convincing human ancestors.

In John's View, the major question to address was their rapid brain development, that increased its capacity by some 500cc from the assumed 900cc of the homo-erectus in mere thousands of years against a backdrop of almost static genetic stability in all other growth and fauna. John knew that a simple fern leaf blew in the earthly breezes of 280 million years ago in pretty much the same form that it does today. He also knew that a fish had been caught up in a net of a fishing fleet, that was thought to be extinct. It looked exactly the same as its predecessors of 400 million years ago.

Indeed, the primary classifications of marine life had established themselves on earth in the so-called Cambrian explosion of 5 to 6 hundred millions of years ago with no preceding fossil history. John saw these as the Pre-Cambrian missing links, and Charles Darwin had no answer to the problem; and 140 years after Origins was published, his profession and its associated branches of science still had no convincing answer for this great fossil discrepancy. It had become clear to John that the reaction by what he assumed were animal rights extremists, was due to their misunderstanding him, thinking he had somehow denigrated the chimpanzees and their lack of intelligence. This was just not so, he had merely pointed out the huge gulf that existed between the greatly over- endowed human brain, in comparison to the extremes of the respective evolutionary time periods of less than one million years in the case of humans, to some fifty million in the case of the primates. John had consigned most of his, what could only be described as hate mail or negative correspondence, to his old-fashioned wicker paper basket.

His assumption that the writers were animal rights extremists was due to the fact that they mostly poured out a tirade of abuse about "the arrogant assumption of certain humans who not only turn a blind eye to atrocious animal experiments, but assume that it might be impossible for themselves to have evolved from them, yet act worse than any animal in their more negative pursuits and continue to slaughter their fellow men in constant and futile wars." John did not wish to keep such letters, but he certainly had to admit, they had a point.

Others seemed to give the impression that they had been waiting for such a book as *The Human Enigma* to appear, to reinforce their own views. He had been struck by one strongly worded reiteration that stated, "all humans that had lived and died over the last century and a half had been the victims of the greatest confidence trick or propaganda exercise in recent history." It wasn't clear to John whether this letter reflected a form of religious mania in the writer, who was greatly disturbed by the Darwinian teachings that disregarded Genesis or was strongly reiterating his own disgust at having possible ape-like ancestors, as either assumption could be formulated, and he did not say he had actually read 'The Human, Enigma'. If he had read it, he had missed the point of its intended impartiality. Many people singled out one aspect of his work and assailed him regarding it, in their letters by going over the top as it were. John had received a few pompous verbal assaults, that in the main, suggested that it was an impertinence for somebody like himself, who was not highly advanced in his profession, to question the works, and their conclusions, of hardworking scholars and academics of long standing, whose industrious efforts had contributed to many widely used textbooks, etc, etc. He had even received sympathetically worded letters, stating that the writer would pray for him, and hoped that he, and everyone else who failed to grasp the true meaning of life, would eventually seek the light of truth and so forth. Certain people among the letter writing group, seemed to pick out one particular aspect of his book and dwell on it as though that was all it was about. Consequently, John worried a little about the forthcoming television programme and the reaction it might provoke.

Although he had actually been to the television studio when it was being produced, he had found that the actual process was quite unlike that which the viewers would finally observe, which of course would be an orderly sequence of events in a naturally flowing programme.

John had travelled to the city by train, and was met by his friend, who would present the show, David Villiers. David was to take him to the studio to observe the making of the programme, and to be on hand to offer any advice or criticism he might feel to be necessary. What bothered John a little, was instead of following the format of his book in simply presenting the problems and unaddressed questions and looking at any kind of evidence that may exist in support of them, he would firstly have to face a barrage of questions by a panel of academic experts behaving as though he had introduced some novel radical theory of his own. John recalled that he had wavered a little as they approached the white impressive Broadcasting House. David Villiers seemed to sense this reticence on John's part, to even enter the building. It must have been his body language that caused David to detect John's apparent apprehension of what was to come, and firmly grasped his elbow. Villiers seemed to give out the impression that in his opinion, John was about to turn and run. John felt the pressure of his grip as he guided, propelled him almost, up the steps of the broadcasting station. "Steady John." He whispered firmly, "don't worry, it will be a piece of cake, they probably won't have to ask you anything, after all; you've said it all in your book, haven't you? Now it's all down to them. They just want you on hand to comment .... you know if you feel that they aren't handling it right, that's all." Nevertheless, John could not completely shake the feeling that he was being led like a lamb to the slaughter. He had remarked to Villiers. "I hope they don't give out the impression that I'm some sort of crackpot eccentric or radical, I'm in enough trouble with my colleagues as it is. And if you saw some of my mail you would know what I mean. I'm not being cross-examined in any way, I made that clear before I did all those other appearances. I don't mind a one to one with a show's presenter, but I don't want some panel of high-minded academics trying to put me on the spot as though I was representative of the lunatic fringe, especially since my book was only an objective presentation of the views opinions and theories already in place for quite some time."

"I simply chose to make it clear that there are many questions to be answered relevant to any theory for human origins, not just the Darwinian View, which in any case, in my opinion at any rate, has become more of a sacred cow than a theory, and it's still not completely proven to everyone's satisfaction. Nothing I have written about is radically different or stated as my own particular viewpoint." As they passed quickly along a corridor, Villiers had replied with a detectable twinkle in his eye. "Look John, with all due respect, you have to put your money where your mouth is sometime, don't you?" This remark by Villiers had only reinforced John's assumption that he was heading for some grand inquisition.

"I know all that," he replied "but the first section of the work only represents the mysteries and anomalies that others in my profession are all well aware of, yet for the most part choose to ignore, or at least seem reluctant to discuss. And as far as the second section is concerned, I drew my data from well-established biblical texts that have been accepted as literal truth by-countless people for centuries. Even the third section, as I have often stated, does not represent my own radical notions or conclusions, and the data that appears to support it," can be accessed by anyone like myself taking the trouble to research it for themselves. I simply related the views and theories of others, that included incidentally, quite a few highly qualified people. I'll bet you don't know that a NASA scientist and a mathematician with a doctorate, jointly produced a book *Mankind, Child of the Stars* in which they seriously suggested in a non-fiction work, that humans are hybrid creations and that the more profound unique qualities of the human brain are due to a bequest from visiting extra-terrestrials, now how about that? "Furthermore," he quickly added, "the late professor Carl Sagan considered the possibility that earth had been visited by another world intelligence long in our past. Even our own sciences, which could be quite primitive in comparison to other more advanced life forms, are busy isolating genes responsible for human intelligence. How do we know that this will not lead to a situation, where humans themselves may well be infusing intelligence into lesser mortals, long into the future, possibly even on other worlds? We can't be arrogant enough to assume that only earthbound science can do these things." John had realised that his voice had gone up a few octaves, as he made all these points to David Villiers, but Villiers, in his calm unflappable manner soon brought it back down again. "You're preaching to the converted old boy. I have read your book you know, so calm down. In any case," he said, grinning widely, "I was only teasing you a little, I'm sorry, I couldn't resist it. The format won't be like what you're expecting at all. I'm the presenter, the anchor man and the grand inquisitor all combined. I've told you, there's nothing to worry about, you'll do this standing on your head." Villiers had side glanced at John, probably thinking that he still remained unconvinced.

"Look," he stated forcefully, "there are experienced people handling this. They all know what they're doing. Okay, there may be a little mediumistic licence, we can't be too stuffy, but nothing will be put in that you will not be aware of. They will give you a transcript and you can review the completed programme before it goes out. But in the main, they will stick pretty close to your book. Trust me, you won't be put on the spot, I promise you."

As it turned out, Villiers had been right. His visit to the broadcasting studio had been 'a piece of cake' as David put it, and not a little confusing, one might almost say boring.

John wasn't used to the routine of the studio, with scenes filmed out of sequence to the format of the book. It had all seemed so disjointed with regard to the compilation. At lunch later, when he discussed this with Villiers, David had explained that it was all simple expediency, based on economies, with an eye on production costs"; There was a jury panel and consequently a lot of extras to feed and water, we couldn't have them coming back and forward every day."

Now the programme was completed, and John had vetted the script and viewed the completed video, less the part where the panel or jury, would come in with their verdict. He was quite satisfied with the professional way in which it had been produced. David Villiers seemed quite polished in the manner of his introduction and presentation of the data. David would be successful in getting the point across to the viewers that although many questions would be shown to exist, regarding a profound subject of high interest to many, it was primarily directed at the layman, and any complicated scientific data regarding gene patterns, and biological questions and so forth, would be the subject of a later programme to follow, where the scholars and academics who were involved in biological sciences and paleo-anthropological studies, would be invited to attend and air their views. After the programme had gone out, they could if they wished, express a desire to attend and either fax, phone or write in as directed. Where any imbalances could be redressed.

The three sections comprising the basic layout of *The Human Enigma* would be presented in turn to the panel. They would be made aware of all the facts, relevant data and evidence, factual or circumstantial, for each belief system. It would be made clear to them that many important - and unanswered questions still remain unresolved, for any theory or assumption held, to explain humankind's appearance on earth. Then, the data and the evidence, circumstantial or otherwise, would be put to them. They would then retire and by dealing only in pure logic, and acting only according to the evidence, they would attempt to reach a verdict, on which assumption for how humans came to be, seemed the most compelling to them as a group. John had made it clear during his Visit to the studio, that he did not wish to be present during the scenes of the verdict, or have it included in his by DVD compilation. He had decided that he would prefer to watch it with his family in the comfort of his own home. When observing the making of the show, he had been intrigued by the reactions of the panel as David Villiers skilfully laid out the data and anomalies regarding each belief system to the seated jury. At certain moments during the presentation, a few panel members would confer, look at each other in surprise, reach for the sheaf of quotations and references in front of them. Eyes would widen here; an eyebrow would be raised there; and it was quite evident that at least a few surprises and revelations of previously unknown facts were being conveyed to them. John's thoughts again returned to the present. He slowly swirled the brandy around in his glass, then glanced at the old-fashioned wicker paper basket that always reminded him of his schooldays. The chalky, dusty woody smell of the schoolroom always returned nostalgically to him when he looked at it. John was fond of rummaging in old buy or exchange bookshops and had spotted the basket in one such outlet among a pile of bric-a brac on sale and couldn't resist it.

The basket was currently full to the brim with crumpled discarded mail of the negative and disparaging kind which he had ploughed through ever since publication of his book. Though now starting to diminish, that kind of letter had made up the bulk of his postbag. He had been aware, during the compilation of the manuscript, that there might be such reaction. Particularly with regard to the section dealing with biblical creation. John had been brought up a Catholic, and though diverting from its rigid disciplines, he still respected its" teachings, and indeed those of any other faith. But hard questions had to be asked when dealing with the obvious clash between pure logic and the doctrines only supported with blind faith. John had hoped that he had dealt with it in as sensitive a manner as he could and was surprised that a certain amount of his letters went over the top as it were. His ego had assured that a fair proportion of his more positive correspondence had been retained and filed away, and indeed reviewed from time to time, in order to help him retain the View that his efforts in writing *The Human Enigma* had not been a complete waste of time.

After receiving notice of publication and particularly when sales began to pick up, John had traversed the entire spectrum of emotions, from pride, elation, doubt, uncertainty, perplexity and anger, even regret and frustration. Most of which, he had been entirely unprepared for. Naturally, he had been elated by the publicity, increased sales, the royalty cheques and the improved lifestyle of himself and his family, but he also had to suffer the slings and arrows of outraged ecclesiastics, his own colleagues, academics and a few who simply signed their letters 'animal lover.' It was this kind of mail that disturbed him the most, as he felt they were unjustified, in the sense that nothing he had written, in any way denigrated animals. He had merely pointed out, largely for those of his own profession, who avidly observe chimpanzee behaviour for human-like traits; that an enormous and insurmountable gulf exists between them and humans in terms of intelligence, and if they wished to see intelligence displayed in animals, they should go to a sheepdog trial or an aquarium that has dolphins.

Before John had arranged for an ex-directory telephone number, he had spent long periods of his time trying not to lose patience, as his anger gradually arose in reaction to the comments of certain callers. Often, with his self-control slowly ebbing away, he would state firmly, "Okay, what part of the book are you referring to specifically?" It had become clear to him that in most cases, the majority of the callers had formed their pre-conceived notions about what he had been attempting to say in his book, from press items, adverse comments, in one case, a newspaper from a certain religious persuasion, adverse reviews and other negative comments, rather than having actually read his book themselves.

This situation had reminded him of an occurrence in the 70's where he recalled that he had been reading about the successful musical *Jesus Christ Superstar*. An outside broadcast team had been present, and after obtaining a few comments from a couple of people in the queue, they moved on to the placard-carrying protesters to elicit reaction from them. They stopped walking up and down and began to gather around the interviewer, all seeming anxious to get their comments across. John read that even a few nuns were among them. The commentator patiently listened to half a dozen of them, then spoke into the camera carried by his partner. Shortly after, the team began coiling up leads and taking their equipment back to their van, and as they passed down the line of queuing people, some had overheard the interviewer saying to the cameraman, "do you know, not one of them has even seen the show!"

John never discussed his, one might almost say hate mail, with his family. He took the view that since he had sown the wind, he would have to reap this particular whirlwind on his own. However, there were many encouraging and positive letters, which he had appreciated greatly. Some pointed out a few facts to him that he had been unaware of, but in the main, they mostly agreed with his view that the widespread open discussion on the unresolved issues had certainly been long overdue. This alone was sufficient justification for his work, even though he had created enemies among some of his colleagues. His only regret was that he had omitted the facts that had been pointed out to him in his more supportive letters.

However, his most cherished letters by far, were those from members of his own profession who now obviously felt their guilt in going along quietly with all the assumption and conjecture when all the time their instinct was telling them to speak out about their doubts and perplexity on why, so many years after Charles Darwin's rather daring assumptions, we seemed no nearer to conclusively proving it all.

It had long been clear to John Willoughby, and, he had assumed, anyone else who took the trouble to study the evidence and its implications and wording of his idea of evolution and natural selection; "ever scrutinising and improving, rejecting that which is bad and adding up and preserving all that is good," is not at all reflected in the scrappy human bone fossil evidence. What seemed more evident was a perplexing disjointed and puzzling emergence of bone fossil portions that raised more questions, rather than providing any answers. A small array of hominid skulls, appearing more like different varieties of primate, in spite of dentition or any other features, and certainly not reflecting a gradually improving process. And although Charles Darwin stuck to his guns, so to speak, his 'co-producer,' as one might describe Alfred Russell Wallace, did not. It seems A.R. Wallace was more reluctant than Charles Darwin to abandon all notions of a higher force, or grand creator, yet Darwin himself appeared to see a 'guiding force' or positive selection, rather than assigning it all to blind chance. For what else but a guiding force could be daily and hourly scrutinising, selecting, adding up and preserving, rejecting, and so forth. Whichever way he looked at it, John himself saw evidence of a 'force.' The problem was to quantify or identify it. John was aware of another view that science was warming to, regarding a few of its members, and that was, that life per-se, on earth, may have simply been a biological accident, and may never be repeated and serves no purpose. This would assume that life due to any other means, has a purpose, but he knew, from his interest in the work of the astrophysicists that life's molecular groups have been and still are, being detected in space, and that this, together with the clear evidence of amino acids being found in meteorites, which one assumes exist in other systems, then as far as John saw it, the ingredients were on the table waiting to go into the bowl. All that would be needed would be a moist temperate world in a similar habitability zone as earth, circling another sun-like star, of which there are a great multitude.

John had considered this alternative view but had not dealt with it in his book as to him it seemed so negative. To be sure, one planet out of nine in our own system with life, cuts down the odds considerably. But, with a little effort, earthly sciences well into the future, will probably ensure that three worlds in our system's eco-sphere will eventually support life. Where earthly eyes have focused on Mars in this regard, and scientific effort brought to bear on that world, Venus was the venue for comic book science fiction stories in the early days as well as Mars, until we found what a hellish place it really is. Whether it was always like that, John felt was open to conjecture. The earth has clearly warmed up according to deep core drilling and temperature measuring techniques, by a full one degree Celsius in the last 500 years, with half of that increase taking place in the twentieth century. In other words, due to the effects of the industrial revolution. Russian science has devoted more time and expenditure in their space activities, to Venus, and seem confident enough to announce, that it too, as well as Mars could be brought to life in not too many centuries. John certainly looked at the life process as a 'force' rather than anything to do with blind chance or 'accidents' happening anywhere. In fact, he saw it as inevitable, given the right conditions. The sheer strength of plants and their roots forcing their way up the tiniest cracks in concrete, and heaving up tarmac a few inches thick, rather like a weight lifter pushing a heavy mass above his head. Any keen gardener knows how he has to fight this force, that would take over the whole garden if he let it. To assign this force to the actions of a divine almighty creator, is largely ignored by scientists, who feel that such a view is mystic and unscientific, and their feeling is, that the force will eventually be defined by, and ultimately explained by the scientific processes. But who is to stand up and declare that the former viewpoint is wrong, when being unable to offer anything better in return?

With regard to the evolutionary force pertaining to humans, it seemed to be rather confused in its idea of just what to produce. It seems virtually impossible to construct a viable and unquestionable family tree, back to any of the strange hominids. Their strange ape-like skulls, cobbled together from hundreds of pieces and finished off with generous amounts of plaster to complete the assumed shape, seem to encourage the view, that if these creatures were alive today, they would be either in the trees or in one of our zoos. This seemed an easier assumption to John, than imagining them fashioning Stone spearheads, particularly the more robust Australopithecines with great sagittal crests and lowering brow ridges. He could not see them as being on a direct line of descent to modern humans at all. With regard to the strange Neanderthals, there was enough data for the publication of a 400-page book, yet the bottom line remained "they remain the subject of conjecture and debate." As far as John Willoughby was concerned, when looking for convincing ancestors, he couldn't get past the anatomically modern Aurignation-Cro-Magnon peoples. In other words, one couldn't even set out on the yellow brick road without unresolved stumbling blocks being immediately confronted, that remain the subject of debate. What then was the force that shape-shifted so rapidly the human skull, to its more modern shape to house the forebrain, the seat of our higher functions? We know so little about the brain, but these convolutions are 'new' areas of the brain. More particularly, the speech centre in the third convolution of the temporal lobe or Broca's area. John knew these areas were nothing to do with Pithecoid alleged ancestors and a brute existence, they govern speech, abstract thought and technical skills. Having a brain with the ability to discover the laws of gravity, tabulate the chemical elements, peer into the smallest particles of matter, invent radio, utilise nuclear power and contemplate interstellar travel, are hardly attributes necessary merely to gather nuts; defend himself against predators and hunt down game. Yet many of his colleagues still see the human as little more than a naked ape. However, John was aware that many of them were equally as perplexed as himself, and more than a little irritated and frustrated in considering the comparative ease in which the whole dinosaur picture, their skeletons and their habitats and life style can so easily be formulated, assembled and analysed, when these creatures expired some 65 million years ago. Yet, the human picture from just a couple of million years ago cannot be similarly dealt with. The odd fossil alleged to be human pops up from time to time that makes our dating methods and techniques appear suspect, as they seem to have no place in that part of the fossil record.

Given the comparatively short evolutionary period of humankind, John felt that one ought to able to walk into any natural history museum and admire a complete array of human skeletons with every ancient bone in place. One ought to be able to walk along this line of skeletons as though walking back in time, and see the spinal column where it enters the skull, moving further and further back, with skulls changing; shape shifting; chests becoming barrel-like, arms lengthening, legs shortening, the body moving down onto all fours as the hip joints changed, yet we haven't a single skeleton that could be described as 100% complete. Why don't the processes of natural erosion uncover such remains when they so ably assist in providing all those bones from so many millions of years earlier. Surely some complete skeletons could have been preserved in clay seams.

It was a perplexing question, and led John to consider that Charles Darwin, if he could somehow return, may admit that he would have to think it out again. But of course, he had been astute enough to insert his built-in 'escape clause' by stating "if the fossil links are not found then the theory falls down." A large proportion of the dinosaur bones were not searched for at all, yet for 140 years we have purposely searched for human remains, and in the most likely places with so little obvious success. Although John knew that many of his colleagues were well aware of these shortcomings and problems existing in the theory, they all seemed to commonly unite on the viewpoint that the entire theory that Charles Darwin himself wavered over, regarding certain points, and his contemporary Alfred Russell Wallace diverted from completely, was entirely and unquestionably correct. It was quite well known that the study of old bones and the work of the paleo-anthropologists, particularly with regard to the correct interpretation of the fossils and their relevance, was the most contentious of all the sciences, and had been ever since its first inception. This committal to the theory was quite understandable for those who had diverted in earlier times from former beliefs, simply because they had nowhere else to turn. Today however, other alternatives do exist, but John knew that it was most unlikely that any of his colleagues would ever consider the third alternative Spelled out in John's book *The Human Enigma*. It seemed rather unfair to him that the science of his profession could dismiss the beliefs of so many people as 'mystic and unscientific,' when so many anomalies, one could almost say mysteries existed, within their own science. However, the difference between John and his colleagues was, that he was prepared to, and actively encouraged others to; face up to these many unanswered questions and anomalies, and this they seemed, for the most part, reluctant to do. Although John agreed that the general format and the manner in which the biblical creation doctrine was presented in the Old Testament story of Genesis, was difficult to accept and made it comparatively easy for science to take that view, there were certain aspects of the story that John had found during his close analysis when completing his manuscript for *The Human Enigma*, that had intrigued him greatly, and certainly provoked further study. He had found some curious references that seemed to indicate a scientific knowledge of the initial life processes and how it began on earth, that were only seriously considered in time periods of many centuries later. Although not claiming to fully understand the process in all its intricacies, science certainly agrees that life seems to have begun in the seas. How then did Moses come by this knowledge? After all, he states in Genesis "Let the waters bring forth the moving creature that hath life." Egyptian priests and scribes related many things to Visiting Greeks and scholars of much later time periods than when Moses lived. They stated that the sun did not always rise in its current easterly point. This could only imply a historic knowledge, possibly only verbally handed down since a time when the earth's tilt was not 23 1/2 degrees or a knowledge of the polar gyrations or so-called precession of the equinoxes, which take some 26,000 years to complete.

John had discussed this interesting anomaly with a few of his colleagues who seemed equally as open-minded and enquiring as himself, regarding this belief System of biblical human creation. But, from which original source came the data recorded in such detail by Moses? Or who told Moses the story? He is stating the words of a divine creative God, not his own. The creation story would of course pre-date Moses and be known even by Abraham, but Moses was allegedly brought up in an Egyptian household after his rescue from his basket on the River Nile and raised as half-brother to Rameses the second. And therefore, he would have received the best Egyptian education possible, and was no doubt tutored by the most knowledgeable scribes.

The ooparts (or out of place artefacts) found in quarry rock and so forth, now began to make some sense. Earthly history could be stood on its head if men were recording knowledge (to be handed down later) when the sun rose in a different place than it does today. Now, all those legends of antediluvian cultures begin to appear more credible. The point John had reiterated was, if Moses was writing words that were scientifically correct, how much more of his Genesis creation story could be scientifically correct, particularly in regard to 'making men?' Shortly, geneticists will 'make' a human heart by cellular reproduction in a laboratory. How long before men will 'make' another human in their own image? Right now, we could clone another Einstein from his brain cells as it has been preserved. A divine creative God would surely not bother with ribs from Adam or bodily material to produce another human where only the gender was changed, by further scientific process; he would simply wave an airy hand and state "Let Adam have a wife." Moses, long before writing the Genesis story, could have spent much of his youth in the great libraries, absorbing knowledge of how men were 'made' by God or lesser gods, as is indicated in all the other earthly legends. John found it a strange paradox indeed, that out of the three sections of *The Human Enigma*, the two that would be the most scientifically rejected, indicate men were 'made' and can point to many factors that add up to a wealth of circumstantial evidence in their favour, yet the most scientifically accepted, struggled to find any answers at all. John knew that it had been academically and scientifically postulated, that the human is a mathematical improbability, and in theory shouldn't exist at all. He is a misfit of evolution and as far as John Willoughby was concerned; and he knew that it distanced him from his colleagues, the isolated splendour of the human brain at its best, in the Einstein's of the world, had nothing whatsoever to do with Pithecoid alleged ancestors. In fact, he went further, and postulated on the idea that Homo-Sapiens should be a separate genus of his own, and not merely one of several species within the genus 'Homo' which currently include Neanderthal and Homo-Erectus types, as it is almost certain they could not have interbred.

John often felt like 'a traitor within' but he knew he could never surmount the stumbling block of the human brain and its profound over-endowments, that so completely defy the processes of natural selection, that simply do not have, nor do they single out 'favourites' for any special treatment.

It was largely due to all his considerations and thoughts along this path that made it easier, not to say rather interesting, to sift and analyse the data for the third section of his book, that at least provided a plausible assumption, if one has at least a modicum of imagination, for such human qualities that the dogma of his own profession fails so dismally to explain.

He had presented the rather substantial amount of factors and circumstantial evidence as impartially as he could, for this third alternative, or belief system, to explain how the unique human came to be. They had existed and had been briefly hinted at and firmly suggested by various writers, decades before John had even considered writing *The Human Enigma*. Nevertheless, it was still a rather fantastic suggestion. It was strange to think that now, many scientists, though largely derisive in their comments, were actually discussing this rather profound suggestion frequently, on an open forum throughout the media and on prime-time television shows, which before had rarely, if ever been the case. As for those who had never encountered this suggestion, who must by now be few, could now at least be given the chance to consider the theory and any evidence that may support it for themselves, even if it was all entirely circumstantial. John felt that in order to simply assess it, one only needs to have an open mind, and consider the many problems, mysteries, anomalies and unaddressed questions that exist in the two primary belief systems for human origins.

Although John believed he had retained his objectivity and impartiality when analysing all the data relative to this rather profound theory. He had to admit that it went some way in offering itself as a candidate for the outside force or some unknown variable, that A.R. Wallace struggled with and which prevented him from accepting the entire Darwinian package. It also fitted in well with John's own particular stumbling block, which was rather akin to that of A.R. Wallace. But if one is to reject the notion of a divine infallible creator, and any notion of a pithecoid ancestor providing the astounding human qualities then what is left to consider? Here, the third alternative steps neatly in to fill the gap.

This anomaly of the explosive development of human intelligence that John called supernatural evolution, could not simply be side stepped or ignored. We must at least make an attempt to explain it or continue our research in order to do so. All those millions of years of obvious genetic stability in every living thing, except the enigma of the human entity, cry out for an adequate explanation.

John had come to realise that there was one topic that was guaranteed to make his colleagues fall silent or change the subject, and that was, the anomaly regarding the great distance apart, that both humans and simian kind stood with regard to the development of their brains and their respective intellectual capacity. In spite of their reaction, John was quite unrepentant in having introduced this third alternative into his book. In the first place he had purposely and quite intentionally included it, primarily, to show that alternative belief systems did actually exist and were open to anyone considering the mystery of human beginnings.

Where science could not adequately explain how a brain so obviously over-endowed normally, has even excess brain cellular material in reserve, and presumably one day to become active, this so-called fantastic theory could. John had conceded all along that it was more appropriate to consider a more rational and scientific approach, before dealing with, and confronting more radical and astounding theories, that seem more like science fiction than scientific and he had done so, even though science had failed him in this regard, he had not abandoned the ship and fallen in behind this third alternative as a substitute. He had simply presented the data that seems to support it, people could make up their own minds. Although he had watched some of the programmes where professional people were at least paying lip service to a subject they would at one time have deemed as untouchable, John had now given up hope of encountering a single argument that could totally refute all the data and circumstantial evidence he had presented in *The Human Enigma* for the third alternative, and this appeared to be its greatest strength. Among the more academic works in his possession, John had an expensive glossy hard-backed publication that made it clear from the start that there were many problems to face for anyone setting out to solve the mystery of human origins, and that many traps were waiting for the unwary. John had always viewed it as a little unfair to admit to all the problems in these academic textbooks that the average layman rarely encounters or seeks out, unless making a specific study of the subject, than, to continually refer to ape- like ancestors and chimpanzee cousins when as far as relatives or ancestors are concerned, we cannot really get past our immediate and only convincing ancestor, the anatomically modern Aurignacion peoples. Anthropology in general, was carrying out a subtle indoctrination of the masses by such references. Also, it is openly speculated that the pro-consul or common ancestor of humans and modern apes actually existed, yet we fail to find any evidence of him and cannot even agree on a time period for his appearance, which has been speculated as anything from 5 to 50 million years ago. Nevertheless, John, for all his consternation, still maintained his view of being committed subject to confirmation and no matter how many theories, mysteries and anomalies there were in existence regarding the subject of human origins, the rigidly held conviction and belief in the Darwinian Theory remained firmly in place.

John's natural inclination was that the answers would, in the long run, emerge from the realms of science and not from any ecclesiastical sources or from the data, as interesting as it was, referred to and cited by those soaked in years of science fiction or *Star Trek* scenarios, and the attached more radical theories and suggestions Yet his major point of consternation remained, in that this fantastic third alternative could explain his own major and particular stumbling block so easily, yet his own profession abjectly failed to do so. And he had certainly made it clear that the third alternative was not only very interesting, but cleared up a lot of questions and it certainly could not be disproven, no matter how much it was ignored it will not simply go away and must eventually be faced With regard to the third section of *The Human Enigma* that John had chosen to call the third alternative, he had encountered a whole raft of interesting and compelling factors that appeared to support this rather profound suggestion. He had found a paperback edition of a book published by two well qualified authors, that looked very closely at the question, and they had suggested in a convincing manner that the human brain could have been the result of extra-terrestrial bio-engineering processes, in some specifically chosen Garden of Eden. Other books and articles hinted at extra-terrestrial activity in biblical times, and it was these references that caused John to minutely analyse all the events occurring in the Old Testament for himself. Regarding biblical close encounters and angels, descending and ascending to and from the sky on their pillars of fire, it was necessary to correctly interpret events that had been accepted and uncommented on for many centuries. Gradually his intended impartiality began to be somewhat disturbed, as this startling proposition began to seem less science fiction like and more worthy of analysis. John was aware that a certain professor had earlier stated that it was possible that the earth had been visited by extra-terrestrials in our past yet spent the rest of his career as an astronomer and exo-biologist, apparently regretting it and deriding and debunking the E.T.H. or extra-terrestrial hypothesis whenever possible. John had found that exo-biologist meant an expert on extra-terrestrial life forms and was not aware that we possessed any. Unless, he mused, the ufologists are all quite right after all and alien bodies exist in some secret area, otherwise it would be a science without a subject. After the learned professor's original postulations, many writers began to point to the numerous and unexplained wonders of the world and began to assign them to the work of visiting extra-terrestrials; and the scene was set to take it a little further and assign the entire process to them also. Of course, he realised that the ET human creation theory had been in place for many decades, and that many earthly legends have a common factor regarding ' God or gods involved in the creation process. And his biblical studies and their possible relevance to the theory, therefore intrigued him the most. One thing was for certain as far as John Willoughby was concerned, and that was, that the human brain at its best, placed the human entity with its short evolution, ahead of any alleged ape-like relatives by an enormous stretch of time. Yet primate ancestry goes back almost 50 million years, and for all that evolutionary time in which to develop a super creative brain, they do not even possess the simple basic ability to peel a banana, unless shown or trained to do so. How an ape-like pro-consul could bequeath such gifts to humanity, when simian creatures have kept so little for themselves caused John's logical processes some concern, but for all that, he still retained the thought that one day the vital evidence will emerge, in order to solve the problems once and for all. But, John was determined to remain open-minded enough to at least consider alternative theories on their merits, and he had to admit that the volume of data he had ploughed through, could easily be seen to indicate something quite profound if one chose to accept its implications as circumstantial evidence with regard to the ET thesis. And so, unlike some of his colleagues, John's interest and field of study embraced all the theories and the entire spectrum of assumptions and belief systems relative to the question of origins. However, he was well aware of the enormous problems involved in taking on board such radical notions. John was not a biologist, but he was possessed with enough common sense to be aware how difficult it would be for a trained biologist to accept this third alternative, that actually proposed that extra-terrestrial entities encountered earth, and after a study of its life forms, set about the business of bequeathing their advanced intelligence genes to some suitable primate recipient. He knew that biologists could and would raise a whole host of reasons to rule it out as sheer science fiction. Nevertheless, John was always irritated by the close-minded blinkered approach, or such statements as biologically impossible, 'unless of course such remarks were, at least, qualified with a few additional words such as biologically impossible for us here on earth today. He felt this was particularly relevant when considering the fact that the scientific members connected with his own ' profession were struggling to finalise their enquiry; and difficulties regarding the initial life process in all its intricacies, from basic matter to cellular reproduction not to mention the missing fossil evidence, in order to put their own chosen theory to bed, so to speak.

Most people were aware, that as long as fifty years ago, certain experiments had taken place producing amino acids in sealed retorts, by sparking a mixture of gases assumed to have existed on earth long ago, with simulated lightning discharges. But, they had never produced the whole range of some 20 amino acids necessary for the life process, and nothing had ever climbed out of the vessel.

Nevertheless, John knew that amazing strides in genetic science and development had occurred since those times, and science was rapidly advancing toward the point when humans themselves may reach a stage that would be seen by the religious factions as a challenge to the divine creator, by becoming creators of life itself by their own advancements. It was also clear to him that the astrophysicists and astronomers were not hostile to the idea of other creative intelligences existing among all that multitude of suns, many of which were quite like our own. And, they certainly spend their allocation of funds for the SETI (Search for Extra-terrestrial Intelligence) programmes, avidly searching for signs of their possible transmissions. And of course, once having accepted the ETH (extra-terrestrial hypothesis), it would seem quite ridiculous to suppose that they would all be less advanced than ourselves. The process then becomes self-generating. If some are more advanced than they could have attained a state of advancement long ago, that we are still striving to reach and may one day also attain. Part of this process would include discovering a practical method or power source, for humans to travel interstellar, rather than interplanetary distances. And so, John concluded that this theory could not simply be dismissed out of hand, even though just getting here would only be the first consideration, and it seemed dangerous not to say a little arrogant, to dismiss this theory with just a few words, such as 'out of the question' or 'impossible'.

And so, in *The Human Enigma* John had simply spelled it out in plain terms what this third alternative was all about, and the many problems that would be associated with it when giving it any consideration. He had immersed himself in all the data, and in doing so, tried to approach it from the scientifically enquiring viewpoint, but he had to free himself from any self-imposed restraints that many sceptics, regarding the whole matter as sheer science fiction, might shackle themselves with mentally.

He quickly disposes of the we can't, so they couldn't attitude. But just how strong was the evidence? He knew that there was no convincing material evident, at least that could be accessed by himself, or anyone else for that matter. It was easy to make a conjecture that flying saucers were being flown, tested and even being built, by analysing captured alien craft in crash retrievals, and building more by so-called 'reverse engineering' processes in some remote area. But other countries have secret development and test centres to develop their defence capability, yet no-one gathers there to spot flying saucers darting about, such as in the so-called area 51 for example. Defence secrecy and remoteness itself, proves very little. John had been surprised to read a U.S. president had stated in response to a question on the subject, that he "had tried to find out but came up against a brick wall," presumably of silence. As leader of the nation and chief of the armed forces, what was to stop him gathering his White House advisors and top military personnel and flying into the alleged area in 'Airforce One' and demanding a conducted tour? John had intended, yet had not so far got around to it, to visit the Austrian museum that was said to house documentation only, since the item had mysteriously disappeared, regarding a machined cube with a groove cut around it and two opposing convex sides, that was said to have been found in a coal seam. Technology from millions of years ago? He had realized of course that this did not necessarily mean an alien technology, and he had read about the so-called 'ooparts' or out of place artefacts that had been found, that suggested a wipe out of past human advancements, just as is often proposed could happen today in various books and films, where an asteroid puts us back in the Stone Age. But what if they were alien artefacts, where are they? Who has obtained them and now salted them away . . . and where? And, more importantly to John's research, if such things exist and are known to be 'not of this earth,' did the creators of such artefacts have any connection with human creation? It was a deep subject and a difficult one to tackle objectively.

John found himself becoming entrapped and immersed in a wealth of theory, postulation, argument and counter argument, but it was comparatively easy to allow all the evidence to fall into place. So, he simply continued to analyse and assess the factors that emerged in the various books and data obtained from the period of a few decades ago up to the more recent publications. As it turned out, it required more effort than the other two sections of his book put together. John was quite aware of the scientific fraternities' reluctance to involve themselves in any theory that could not be tested, yet almost to a man, they completely embraced the theory of Darwinian human evolution in its early introduction, when no evidence in support of it existed at all, that could be tested. And today, any testing they do carry out, for example, regarding the DNA of human blood and mitochondrial DNA, bedevils the theory completely and indicates a more recent origin for humankind. And so, in terms of sheer logic, John therefore took the view that if Charles Darwin could get away with such a breath-taking assumption that gorillas and chimpanzees were man's closest living relatives, when not a single ancient bone existed, then be completely embraced by science, then what is the difficulty of an equally breath-taking assumption, of an alien intelligence altering human evolution, being at least considered briefly when at least some evidence, albeit circumstantial, can be mustered in its favour? Nevertheless, John did not wish to become a mentor or spokesman or write as though he was an authority on the subject of the third alternative, but simply to present it as a belief system that many people did subscribe to as that was the sole purpose of *The Human Enigma*, no more, no less.

If alien biogenetic creation was the common denominator or bottom line, then the supporting factors could quite easily be added to the equation to make it work, so to speak. But as well as spelling out the theory as a belief system, it had been necessary to also present the problems and factors to his readers as to why scientists, in the main, distanced themselves from it. Most people were aware, that science in general was quite predisposed to the possibility of another world intelligence existing, but just to get here and discover earth and its enormous variety of life forms would be astounding enough, let alone experimenting with early pre-human DNA. It would have required major advancements in the development of suitable power sources to make interstellar journeys feasible in terms of alien life support, if they were to set up their alleged bases on our moon, under the sea, or in the polar regions, all of which have been suggested by the ufologists. We ourselves could not envisage moon bases on a world only a quarter of a million miles away after frequent visits there by the Apollo team, because of the problems that all multi-cellular life forms encounter in their abject necessity for water and how to get it there. Now, the possibilities open up again with the recent discoveries by analytical probes, that it might exist, locked up in the rocks there. Of course, aliens coming to earth would find a world 2/3 water, but could their body forms take it? Also, visiting aliens would not only have to be well versed in the DNA of their own life form, but also be expert in manipulating ours. And, cellular fusion, microbiology, perhaps even that of other worlds they may have discovered. And of course, all the other sciences, not least, that of mathematics, for such interstellar voyages to be accurately navigated. However, no-one could disregard the possibility that beings could actually exist, that had solved all these problems and more, when earth, had literally been, at one point in its history, a mere planet of the apes.

For all that, John was aware from his interest in the works of the astrophysicists and astronomers that our own star, the sun, is middle-aged yet still had some 4.5 billion years of life left in it. He also knew that other suns had already spent their lives and expired, some in quite a catastrophic manner. And their fast spinning remnants were bleeping out their signals for future interstellar navigators in a frequency as accurate as atomic clocks.

If an intelligence had developed and advanced up to the point of its stars' demise, one could ask, where are all these people? If they possessed the ability as they should have, to leave their world for younger stars such as our own neighbourhood, they should have discovered earth long ago. John knew that any such opposition could be countered by further suggestion, perhaps that such ET's had already arrived and established themselves in earthly habitations long ago. Being clever enough to do all the things postulated, particularly any involvement in our own appearance on earth, they could well be clever enough to keep their presence from being conclusively proven by humans. It was obvious to John, that the very first consideration by any visiting ET's, both in the past or more recently, would be the threat, not only to themselves from our microbes, but possibly their own, affecting any humans that they whisked up into their craft in the form of abductions, to analyse. John had reflected sometimes, during his analysis of the whole problem, that it would indeed be easier to take the path of many of his contemporaries and simply dismiss it all as impossible, and in order to continue, he had to keep uppermost in his mind, that this attitude would prove nothing other than to display obvious 'earthbound' thinking relative only to our own state of technological advancement.

John had to conclude, that in order to seriously consider this theory of biogenetic alien creation regarding humanity, one had to envisage supremely advanced creatures, so far ahead of us in their technology, that in order to explain it to us it would be like modern humans trying to teach a hominid how to build a nuclear power station.

John had to smile whenever he watched the science fiction scenarios depicted on television, of human crews beaming down onto newfound worlds. Simply because they had breathable air and were not only encountering human looking inhabitants with similar accents, but that everyone seemed quite oblivious to the problems that would be encountered with regard to otherworld (and quite alien) microbes, not only in their body forms but in the food and drink they were usually offered. As for the alien atmosphere, they rarely seemed to wear any kind of protective masks or breathing apparatus, just their smart uniforms and phasers.

John was surprised that this problem had never been considered by the many writers and theorists that had put the case that the biblical entities, accepted by, and given due reverence by the Patriarchs as angels may have been aliens, simply because they quite often ascended and descended on pillars of fire in front of the patriarchs, and often conversed with them and partook of earthly food and drink. Of course, if these angels were the descendants of the early creators of humanity, perhaps they had long ago solved these problems. In the second part of *The Human Enigma*, John had carried out a minute analysis of Genesis and The Old Testament and unlike many, with the possible exception of theology students, had read it as one would a novel or textbook. He knew that it had its roots in much older texts and verbally handed down accounts and was therefore more valuable to him in his research than the New Testament, which was in fact the Christian bible. It was the Genesis story and what followed it, that he wished to research. He had realized from such analysis of the Old Testament and the activities of the 'angels,' that it was comparatively easy to assign an extra-terrestrial interpretation to them which was indicated particularly in their 'modus operandi.' They certainly were not described by the Patriarchs as flapping about with golden wings and possessing halos and long white apparel. The Patriarchs had no relative technology to enable them, either to consider that the area above their heads was anything other than heaven, or that descending on a pillar of fire could ever be achieved by humans. And so, they dutifully fell on their faces in awe when encountering them, but did not run away in horror, therefore the angels must have appeared quite human-like and moderately attractive, without any space suits or grotesque looking breathing apparatus to frighten people away, as depicted in science fiction 'B' movies of the fifties. John's first considerations had to be; did the Patriarchs themselves actually and historically exist? If it was yes, were all the biblical characters pathological liars? If this seemed unlikely, were the angels and their various activities involving all the different characters in the bible, figments of the imagination or pure literary license? After that, it only seemed necessary by analysis of their activity, to correctly interpret their real identity, and after such analysis John had found it extremely difficult to assign them the title 'divine.' John as well as everybody else, knew that as a natural course of our own advancement on earth, we had to begin somewhere in our discovery and analysis of earthly bacteria, microbes and diseases, and that no doubt we will eventually amass a complete array of necessary antidotes. And, no doubt, isolate all the human genes for every earthly human trait, fault or malady. Clearly, far in the future, it may also be possible to do so on another world and its array of life forms. Therefore, it was comparatively easy and quite logical, to at least postulate that other more advanced forms of intelligence had long ago done so and possessed the various antidotes and remedies and developed immunization methods against any alien bacteria they may have encountered. They could have enormous catalogues of information stored away in their super computers' memory banks. There was nothing in John's view, that needed to be seen as sheer science fiction, which of course, has often become science fact on earth. One only had to consider the ultimate results of, and where, our own medical science and technological advancements were taking us.

With regard to his analysis of the biblical angels John had to consider the possibility that they themselves could also have been a 'hybrid' creation. If such hypothetical alien 'creators' could find earth and enhance our own intelligence, then their body forms would no doubt be evolutionarily advanced on a par with their technological state of advancement, and though 'humanoid,' they may well fit the description of the so-called greys, with large skulls, and possessing full neuronal capacity, unlike humans built for manual labour tasks, and not yet fully utilizing their total brain cellular material. Such beings would indeed have alarmed the Patriarchs and having the ability in the first place, it would be a natural consideration for them to also create emissaries to achieve their aims and act as acceptable 'angelic' directors of humankind and appear in human-like form to achieve their ends. John began to realize that there were so many features that interconnected between all the subjects of his book, that he found his research began to indicate many components of a wider scenario that may simply culminate in the same conclusion. His next consideration was, could it also have been quite apparent and perhaps already concluded behind closed doors as it were, by some government appointed body? The various authorities such as existed within the Pentagon, the CIA, the MOD, in sections DI55 and S4 (air) for example, or in the often-quoted Area 51? Had some super computer analysis taken place there also? From his knowledge and studies within his own profession, John was aware that the human fossil record was so disjointed and unnatural when attempting to relate it to any 'gradually improving' hypothesis, that it was more akin to evidence of some purposeful creative experiment than a natural process. When he began his studies of the Genesis belief system he found it possible to consider that the emissaries or angels, could have been the descendants of the creators that stated, "let us make men in our image," and did so in some secret earthly location they called Eden. He certainly found it easier to interpret them as aliens rather than angels. Furthermore, during his compilation of the third alternative, and studies of the alleged abductions, he found that two separate and distinct life forms are described by the abductees. Thinly built creatures with large skulls and eyes and more human-like beings that in biblical times would probably be interpreted as angels. It was at this point that his common denominator began to emerge, and John began to struggle to maintain his objective impartiality regarding it all, as piece after piece fell into place. One thing was clear to him, after his deep analysis of the Old Testament and all that activity by the angels, was that they were far removed from the accepted view of them depicted on our Christmas cards, and anyone who took the trouble to review their activities and description in the Old

Testament, would obviously come to the same conclusion. Another prominent feature of the Old Testament that was quite apparent to him, was its complete contrast to the New Testament, with its admirable doctrines and teachings, that reinforced the ideals of The Commandments rather than the events he had read of in the Exodus accounts for example, where angels directly encouraged and involved themselves in the annihilation of masses of humanity and coolly, quite often disregarded the commandment "Thou shalt not kill." During his analysis of the continuing human abduction cases, which even occurred in writings and deciphered tablets predating the bible, it had become obvious that such ongoing abductions, if they followed the same pattern, would indicate an ongoing study of human development over many generations. Which of course was just another of the many pieces of the jigsaw he found neatly falling into place and tending to form a larger picture. John recalled one interesting case of a fairly recent abduction claim he had encountered, that involved a forestry worker in the USA. He had described two separate entities in the version John had read. The victim was indeed alarmed when encountering the thin spindly Greys as he had found was the parlance commonly used by the ufologists to describe them. Then, in order to calm him down and more effectively deal with him, two human-looking individuals appeared, who had one rather obvious difference to the accepted human form, and that was their golden hazel eyes. In other words, beings that the biblical Patriarchs could have encountered and interpreted as angels.

John Willoughby with all his rationality, could sympathize with a scientist who, even though wishing to study all the aspects of the phenomena, would doubt that he stood any chance of obtaining a grant to do so. Equally, he could quite understand the interest of all those people who found it so absorbing and compelling.

John also realized that the entire UFO phenomenon, which was the subject of so much analysis on its own, could also be viewed as another piece of this apparent wider picture. In all the alleged encounters, whether close or far off, and of whatever kind or classification they came under, they could not all be dismissed as physical but misunderstood natural phenomena, dancing lights or ball lightning; as some reports suggested controlled structured craft, and quite often, sightings of the occupants. John was not too convinced by the assumption of those who felt wise enough to say, that if another world intelligence did exist, they would not be likely to resemble us. An ET intelligence may exist alongside many other creatures just as we do on earth. In this assumption then, they may of course be right. But, if another planetary life form existed that was creatively intelligent and the dominant species, and living among an equally wide divergence of other creatures on their world, then it is also logical to assume, that since the life force or evolutionary process on earth seemed to be striving toward bipedalism, and providing free arms and hands with manual dexterity and manipulative fingers, which really seemed to be an evolutionary ideal then it may do so there as well. John took the view that since the list of elements seemed quite short and was probably finite, and also the range of atomic and subatomic particles were universal, then many factors connected with the life force, could also be universal. The predominant material of the universe was hydrogen. If planets have formed around the enormous amount of sun-like stars that can be detected, then during their planetary formation, the same material that was blasted out in atomic structures from the first-generation exploding stars, would exist in them just as it does in the earth. The iron and heavier elements would be gravitationally drawn in, to produce an iron or molten iron core. The soil would also be quite similar, as would their $H2°$, rainfall, weather systems and so forth. The life process could have begun in precisely the same way it is assumed to have done on earth. This view is reinforced by the fact that meteoric fragments do show the existence of such amino acids that exist on earth. If our life forms are the result of 20 basic amino acids and 18 of them could be detected in a meteorite that landed in Murray, Kentucky USA, then the same 20 could be present on another world without too much coincidence.

If such basic building blocks required for life, resulted in lightning striking our ancient seas, then it could quite easily happen elsewhere, and the later photosynthesis processes on the planetary surface may be equally similar on another world to that which occurred on our own planet.

Even the microbes and problems of their differences, and also the possible detrimental effects, could all be overcome. We can genetically modify our food and produce hybrids on a smaller scale ourselves. Every time, John came back to the same conclusion, that it was only a question of the current level of technological advancement that prevailed on any hypothetical otherworld.

John knew that medical science was advancing so fast it even astounded those actively involved in it themselves. He had watched a television programme where a head of a living monkey had been transplanted onto another monkey's body and lived. The surgeon felt sure the time was right to do it on a human life form and astonishingly, made it clear that he might go ahead and do so, ethical restraints or not. Since it was around ten years ago when he had watched the programme, he wondered if it had in fact already occurred. How many human bodies have been donated to science? Where did they go? Who has worked on them? What have they achieved? Where was it done? Do they present an exact list of their actions to the relative who donates the cadaver? John remembered a chirpy comedian whose brain was obviously so alert and active while his body virtually decomposed around him. First one leg becoming gangrenous and being amputated, then the other, then the spreading to the rest of the body. No doubt he would have readily agreed to have been the recipient of a body on a ventilator, where the skull had suffered irreparable brain damage, yet the bodily functions remained normal. Has micro-surgery really advanced that far he thought. He knew about hands being stitched back on and so forth, but to attach a head seemed fantastic with all it implies regarding the spinal cord and so forth. He had recalled checking the calendar to ensure it wasn't April the first, then could see no other reason for a hoax, since the particular programme on that particular television channel quite often dealt with scientific subjects.

Another factor that slotted neatly into place when researching for his third section of *The Human Enigma* was the rather coincidental similarity of all the earthly legends from so widely dispersed land masses. Why would every earth legend be telling men they were made by sky people or gods People might be tempted to smile if they heard a tribal elder relating through an interpreter on a television programme, that gods created their forefathers by coming down from the sky, without considering that the Christian bible teaches the very same thing? It even retains the statement in the plural "let us make men in our image". Even if they call their place of origin Heaven, then they still came from a place other than earth and descended from our sky and made men in a specific zone on earth that biblical legend calls Eden. After his lengthy scrutinizing and analysis of all the data, John had to conclude that it must be difficult for one to stand up and declare that this third alternative was impossible, and indeed every advancement made on earth, would only tend to reinforce it. He had also considered the possibility that inherited memory genes may have been responsible for humans to have reinvented things that previous beings discovered long ago. But whether these intelligent ancestors may have been human ones in some long-lost previous civilization, or were extraterrestrials donating intelligent genes to emerging humans, would be a matter of conjecture. How could earlier primitive humans conclude that it was necessary to extract brown powder out of the ground, to make the first giant leap for mankind and start manufacturing hard metal artifacts? What logical connection existed from just observing the powder? The second giant leap was of course the refining of this ability to manufacture the metal into a space craft, and the third, of course, occurred in July 1969 on the moon with the landing of Apollo 11.

It seemed quite incredible to John that some of his contemporaries could stand back in amazement when observing a chimpanzee stripping the leaves off a twig to poke an ant's nest, when trying to observe human-like traits in their behavior, after 50 million years of evolution, when in the blink of an eye in comparison to that period of time, humans have progressed from bleeding patients in the infirmaries for every ailment, to making statements that we will soon be producing human hearts by cellular reproduction in laboratories. And then go on to assume that the amazing human brain was a simian bequest. Professional people who had made a study of the many cases of alleged human abductions, seemed quite convinced that their subjects were often rational and intelligent people, and it seemed unlikely in their view that such widely separated cases, all of a similar nature, could all be figments of the abductees' imagination. The victims always chose to accept that their abductors were living entities, and not some kind of cybernaut or robotic creature, and in one case, one carried out some form of mind scanning and becalming technique by bringing its head close to the head of the abductee. The calming technique seemed to work, but the perpetrator had little concern about passing on any alien microbes or being infected by any human ones; making its interpretation as living immediately suspect, if not the whole event, which in spite of their alleged widely separated areas, could all be from the heads of the abductees themselves. After all, although ET's could immunize themselves, they couldn't immunize the world's population. If the abductions were true it would be profound enough, but nevertheless could still just be a significant factor in a wider scenario relative to human origins itself. The craft and its occupants would then most likely have to be operating from well-established bases, or earthly locations that may have been set up by their predecessors on earth, or those that stated so long ago "let us make men in our image," and did so in a zone that we know as Eden.

Of course, John was also receptive to the possibility that another world intelligence could encounter earth, that had nothing whatever to do with humans. In that situation only, a few human abductions would be necessary, perhaps just a few examples of the primary classifications of humans. That is, Negroid, Asian and Caucasian. In this case, the craft where the alleged examinations and removal of human genetic material took place, would hardly be interstellar, but a larger craft may be, i.e., some remote mother ship, from which they could be operating. John had read of psychiatrists hypnotically regressing alleged abductees, to elicit their experiences from them. This had happened in one convincing case from the sixties, where the victim almost jumped out of his chair in fright when reliving the experience. But no matter how convincing, the results were, those controlling the process, rarely if ever, believed their patients and assumed they were simply reliving a dream. Which made John wonder why they bothered to do it in the first place.

When assessing the amazing rate of human advancement in medical science, which included the isolating of a gene after a six-year search, that governs intelligence, he found it quite easy to envisage a scenario where humans would be, after further discoveries in this area, in a position to do exactly what this third alternative suggests was responsible for the human race. And in the absence of any evolutionary tendency to do so, enhance the intelligence of a primate. In spite of his contemporaries eagerly pointing out similarities in the DNA of chimps, medical science would still see enormous obstacles to overcome to achieve it. Also, they still turn to pigs when requiring genetic material for human heart operations, and not the chimpanzees. And most people must be aware that the simple infusion of human genetic reproductive material into a chimpanzee would never produce a quasi-human halfway stage, because of the different chromosome pattern. This of course, determines the species, and prevents the chaos that would result in inter species copulation; which is also a major stumbling block as to how all those major changes of species from lungfish to human could actually have occurred, even though it is convincingly displayed in animated films and drawings that theorize how it all happened during the accepted evolutionary process.

John slowly came down to earth from his reverie and looked down at his own copy of *The Human Enigma*. John had a lot to thank his friend David Villiers for. Or more specifically his wife, as it was her brother who was the publisher responsible for his book. David had shown an interest in his other manuscripts and had advised him to seek the services of a literary agent, especially one who could assist in possible film rights. David felt that one of his manuscripts might open up some opportunities for him in that regard.

After publication, his book sales seemed slow to gather momentum at first, now however a certain event had caused it to be featured in the most prominent position of the major book selling outlets and he received frequent requests for personal appearances and book signing sessions. His distributors industriously packaged and sent out their book orders as fast as they could receive them from the printers. This change in John's fortunes with regard to his book sales, came about partly due to a radio programme discussing interesting new publications, but mainly, and ironically due to a chance and quite disparaging remark on a popular TV chat show, by a well-known guest. The TV show obviously enjoyed such good ratings that millions of people immediately had their attention drawn to the subject of his recently published book. And thereafter, sales began to pick up very noticeably.

The TV guest had been a rather cynical 'down to earth' type, who was also an astronomer with quite conservative non-radical views. When the subject of discussion changed to cosmic events, UFO's and so forth, the guest had dryly remarked "all those writers like Von Däniken and now this John Willoughby fellow, who ought to know better than to talk about all this way-out stuff." At that point the host had cut in and said "If I may stop you there... I'm sure we've all heard of Von Däniken, but who's this John Willoughby chappie?"

Although John had read through some of the books by the author referred to and found them interesting and supportive of the subject of his third alternative, John had encountered authors who had written about it earlier, such as Robert Charroux and others, and of course the theory of an outside influence or ET involvement in human origins had in any case, been in place for decades. Although John was perfectly happy with the after effects of this remark, he did not wish to become known as that kind of writer only, which the TV guest appeared to assume or at least imply. Furthermore, John thought that he had made it perfectly clear in his work that all the data in his book had already been written, postulated upon or compiled, before him, and existed in biblical texts, paleo-anthropological works, and the various publications from the period when ancient astronauts were in vogue, and contained no radical ideas of his own at all. He had simply marshalled all the data into three distinct belief systems subscribed to, for how humans came to be and people who read it could simply make up their own minds on which one suited their own particular preference.

For all that, he had to conclude that many subsequent buyers, responsible for the apparent surge of interest and increased sales that ensued directly as a result of that remark, were specifically interested in that kind of material. Moreover, it was quite evident from certain TV programmes dealing with subjects of that nature, that their ratings were sufficiently attractive to ensure their continual return to the television screens from time to time. Clearly, many people are interested in subjects that science avoids, debunks, side steps or ignores completely, simply because that's far easier than attempting to explain them. UFO's, ghosts, paranormal phenomena, all come within this category of untouchable subjects when to many people, it would seem logical for enquiring scientists to adopt quite the opposite attitude. But of course, the old problem of finance and the fact that scientists have to eat too, comes into the frame. John could not imagine any sympathetic scientists setting up a group called Ghost Busters Inc., having much hope of obtaining a research grant.

John had obtained and read a few of those monthly or quarterly productions and knew about B.U.F.O.RA., M.U.F.O.N, and flying saucer review, even a periodical called *Alien*. In his study of them, he bad noticed what one might describe as a ufological fashion trend, namely, the description of the craft now being observed and interpreted as UFO,s Flying saucers are out. Now, the triangular shape is in vogue and everyone appears to be seeing flying triangles. It had occurred to John that if the alleged longevity of the UFO phenomenon is a fact and the flying shields referred to in ancient records were alien craft, then their technology has advanced by a couple of millennia. However, certain things may remain in the optimum design simply because nothing could be envisaged that is better. We couldn't improve on the wheel for example, it is always going to be round. Of course, their sources of propulsion could be enormously advanced since the days of the flying carpets and flying shields and possibly of the disappearances observed by earthly craft when sent to investigate them. It had been theorized that they employ dematerialization techniques. One well written book on the phenomenon that he had acquired, set out to explain this in a scientific manner and spoke of mass field generation to achieve a massless condition by imposing an anti-mass field on the craft. As it was a structured craft and had mass, it had, as everything with mass is alleged to have; a 'mass field.' The purpose of the revolving rim of the saucer was to generate an 'anti-mass' field and consequently achieve invisibility. As this would be difficult to achieve with a triangular shape, it was anyone's guess how they manage to disappear today and become free of inertial and gravitational effects. He had noticed that the UFO magazines seemed to follow the same format as the books on the subject in highlighting the convincing cases, but John saw the entire UFO phenomenon as simply one piece in a much larger scenario, which was of course this third alternative suggestion for human origins.

John recalled that he had worried a little over the best method of approach in dealing with the subject, which was rather a sensitive issue, when compiling the second part of his book, namely biblical human creation of the Genesis kind. It had to be dealt with respectfully as many people still adhere to it in spite of the cold onslaught of science challenging their views in favour of a theory still not fully proven to everyone's satisfaction itself.

John's research was confined largely to the writings of the Old Testament, more specifically the Genesis account. The rest of the research was relative to the activities of the strange beings accepted by the Patriarchs as divine angels. He knew that in studying the first and second books of Genesis, he was digesting the words of a fallible man and not God himself. He also knew that the very existence of Moses had been disputed by certain writers and historians.

However, not everyone who retained Christian beliefs, would describe themselves as tending toward such views through simple blind faith, they had looked at alternative theories and found them wanting. This of course, is reasonably easy to do, regarding the Darwinian concept, and a certain author in the USA had pointed out that Charles Darwin was an amateur in the sense that he did not teach in a university or work in a laboratory. He simply did science in his own home, with none of the elaborate fossil equipment of today and no trained staff to assist him. He also pointed out that people sense a higher presence and that the Darwinian argument is not strong enough to divert them. As for the theory of extraterrestrial existence in earth space and any interaction of humans with them, they need only ask for a single item of tangible proof in the form of an artifact not of this earth to be displayed to them.

Nevertheless, during his entire Catholic upbringing and the intense programming he had had, one could almost say 'bullied' him, he had never once read the Old Testament himself. Now that he had studied it in depth, he could not possibly see how the actions of the angels, not only with their interactions with Moses and his senior staff, but with Abraham in other works, could be interpreted as divine.

Most of their activity seemed to be confined to killing and destroying. Either by eliminating iniquitous cities and their occupants or annihilating Egyptian first born, or killing the enemies of Moses and his followers

As these angels interacted with many different biblical characters in various locations, it wasn't possible to deduce that they were all suffering from the same hallucination. One common feature of all the encounters was the distinct absence of wings and halos. These entities chose to ascend and descend on pillars of fire.

The admirable doctrines of the New Testament were a different matter. Yet the entire religious viewpoint with regard to human origins, was written off by science as mystic and unscientific. In *The Human Enigma*, John had made the point, that where he had shown such respect for the beliefs in Christian teachings and the right of people to retain them, an equal amount of respect should surely be afforded to the atheistic viewpoint also, and of course, the right of such people to reject such doctrines if they feel they cannot accept them. He had asked how such a person would view the entire concept of a divine infallible being, coming along, who had always existended and by the wave of a majestic hand, completes a process, that science feels they have proven, took anywhere between twelve and twenty billion years; in seven days? Nevertheless, his purpose in writing *The Human Enigma*, was not to set himself up as some form of inquisitor regarding biblical writings and their interpretation, but to concentrate on the main points of creation of the human being and in this regard, the strange paradox was that as Adam and Eve seemed to be anatomically modern and fairly attractive humans, this agreed with the fossil evidence. And, the genetic evidence in the appearance of the anatomically modern Cro-Magnon peoples. But try as they might, it would be very difficult for anyone to envisage an almighty creator producing humankind only a mere 50 thousand or so years ago, or that Adam and Eve were the ugly hominid creatures.

Having dispensed with his notion from his early youth, by his biblical studies, that angels fitted the usual description on our Christmas cards of rosy cheeked cherubs, he set himself the task of interpreting their real possible identity. These angelic depictions, that are conjured up in people's minds, usually at Christmas time, are probably due to the religious artists of the Middle ages, who in John's view had never read the Old Testament in detail, as he certainly could never again view them in such a way.

One particular event he had encountered in Old Testament studies was a rather horrifying event, where an angel, in this case, an Angel of death, coldly annihilated, not only Egyptian first born, in the events leading up to the Exodus story, but their parents' cattle as well, which of course was how one's wealth or standing was measured it those times. This angel that passed over the houses of the Hebrews, had by some inexplicable means, the ability to see clearly into all the houses in order to achieve its mission of annihilation. Its only problem was, that it needed positive identification in the form of bloody crosses in order to prevent the accidental annihilation of Hebrew children. John had to conclude, that this process or activity seemed more akin to some unknown mysterious, not to mention cold and cruel technology, rather being angelic or divine in nature. For in terms of sheer logic if it was the latter, then its divine capabilities would not have required such Simple and rather crude identification methods, it would have been quite well aware who was who, in the first place. Strangely, this rather barbaric event is celebrated as something good to remember. John had been intrigued by the entire Exodus story, which of course, Hollywood and the film industry had already exploited to full effect with their special effects technology in biblical epics.

As it had been John's first close analysis of any biblical writings, he had been rather alarmed at further brutalities spelled out involving angels. Particularly one example, where an angel clearly directed the Hebrews before a battle, to "let not a creature that breathes to live." Moses clearly writes of the butchery of men women and children, even their cattle in their battles. John felt that if he questioned a theologian on these matters, the reaction would be that one shouldn't take the writings seriously, but what about all the other events? On this line of thinking, one would, considering the many other events in the bible concerning angels and their activity, finish up being unable to take the entire Old Testament seriously.

Apart from theological students, who probably interpreted these events in their own way, and who must of necessity, closely analyse biblical writings, John had often wondered how many people had actually read the Old Testament meticulously as one would a book? Then went on to attempt some serious analysis of it all. He knew many, like himself, during their schooldays, had never actually read the bible at all, yet some went on to serve mass as altar boys, droning out their parrot-fashion Latin phrases when assisting the priest and some went on to become priests later themselves. It was possible to assume, many people must have lived and died who had considered themselves God fearing and devout yet may never have read a word of these strange events involving the angels. John knew, that this would be so in his own case, simply because if it hadn't been necessary, to Closely study these events in compiling his third alternative he would know nothing about them. He couldn't find any middle ground when considering them. If they were true, they would be very profound, and they could very well be, simply because so many different events and locations are involved. It would be comparatively easy to write them off as literary license, if they only involved one biblical location or character or one story, but they occur throughout the entire Old Testament.

Many authors, especially in the 70's made references to them in the multitude of paperbacks dealing with the ancient astronaut era of those times. But they rarely used more than one or two quotes from certain biblical texts. Although he guessed it had happened in the United States, John had never encountered any locally published books that dealt exclusively with their role on a fully developed thesis in their correct identity or relevance to human origins. And so, John had found it comparatively easy to interpret them as aliens rather than angels. Particularly in regard to their amazing method of ascending and descending on pillars of fire to and from some point in the sky, which he had to deduce was some form of platform, suspended structure or craft. Although the Patriarchs were happy to assume the angels were ascending and descending from Heaven, they must have been curious enough to at least peek through their fingers once or twice as they lay on the ground in awe of them. What did they see? Did the craft have the ability to spray a fine superheated water mist around it to disguise it as a cloud? John had read a rather fantastic story about an allegedly true occurrence during the Gallipoli campaign, where a regiment marched up a hill and disappeared into a cloud that was said to have been observed to move off against the wind. John felt himself becoming deeply immersed in all this data, that continually threatened his impartiality and preference for objective analysis. But in order to logically analyse it, this risk was all part of the process, or the alternative would be to simply write it off as sheer science fiction or nonsense. This, to John would be simply taking the easier course and avoiding the issue completely.

These angels, that obviously required solid food and drink and often did partake of it with the Patriarchs, also communicated with them in their own language and firmly directed them, led them, and fed them with manna from some moving object above their heads, and also provided special instructions for them to produce a special weapon, so lethal to the enemies of Moses and his followers that if they merely touched it, they fell down dead. The angels frequently carried out implants on earthly females to produce special beings such as giants, and the well-known character Samson, with superhuman qualities. John had to consider that these beings were from the same race of creatures that decided "let us make men in our image," so long beforehand. Simply because they took so much interest in humanity, almost as though humans *were* their 'property.' He decided that all this activity in the Old Testament, when read from a modem day technologically advanced viewpoint and our own scientific advancements, that these events were equal to any science fiction story ever written.

John recalled watching a James Bond movie with his two sons, where the hero escaped by strapping on a one-man jet pack and roaring up on a pillar of fire. Not realizing at the time, that it was no special effects stunt but a paid double, utilizing a piece of equipment that had actually been developed for the U.S. marines. Later, during his biblical analysis he realized how profound it was that beings from Heaven, in other words from a place not of this earth, were doing just this so frequently over 2,000 years ago on earth in front of humans.

John came back to reality, focused on his surroundings and realized he was about to tip his drink on to the carpet. He finished it off then glanced at his glass fronted bookcase. In neat rows stood scores of paperbacks he had found by scouring the old bookshops spacemen in the Ancient East? The Flying shields, Was Jesus an Astronaut? Prior to discovering them and their common theme, he had not realized how many books on this subject hinting at extraterrestrial creators of men, had been rolling off the presses a couple of decades ago. Out of all this material that he studied, the book he had mentioned to David Villiers came straight to the point on the subject and was of particular interest to John in that it dealt specifically with his own perplexity, in relating the more profound human mental abilities of such people as Newton and Einstein and many other human geniuses, with any alleged simian ancestor. It had been written by two obviously qualified and quite learned people. One was a mathematician with a doctorate and the co- author was a N.A.S.A. scientist. It had been developed into a book from little more than a paper, titled 'On tiptoe beyond Darwin.' The authors clearly stated that in their measured opinion, mankind may have had super intelligent ancestors from outer space and that humans may be hybrid creations and they presented an interesting and thought-provoking case in their book.

It was entirely due to all these illuminating suggestions, postulations and data, that made John realize that an abundance of material in the form of circumstantial evidence, did in fact exist in such volume, that he could quite easily marshal it all together to purposely produce a third alternative for human origins, in order to show that one need not be slavishly chained to any theory and that other alternatives are indeed open to us.

Of course, he was well aware, that no matter how much data was presented that appeared to support this third alternative, sober detached scientists would distance themselves completely from it, without question. Even deride it yet being unable to offer anything viable in return that could completely dismiss it, or any of the theories and postulations presented in the collection of books adorning his cabinet, alongside his more expensive and academic works. John was often perplexed and quite irritated, that with the obvious advancements in our own medical science particularly in genetic engineering, that science in general, could be so closed-minded to such postulations made by so many people, that only earthly scientists, and no other world beings could have ever achieved long ago on some other planet, the things that they have achieved or state they will shortly be able to accomplish, such as growing of human organs, even the heart, in laboratories. The advances in biotechnology and genetic engineering and isolating genes, that were so obviously occurring today, must surely make at least one or two of them, especially those taking part in the S.E.T.I. programme, consider whether it had all been done before on some other world. It must be seen as an enormously arrogant viewpoint to write off any suggestion of previous alien technologies when many suns have spent their lives and expired, before our solar system formed. However, they are entitled to ask, where are all these people? John had found that this question was known as the Fermi Paradox. And so, he began to write his third section, after compiling all the interesting data and occurrences that appeared to support a third alternative, in a rather bemused and detached manner and simply presented the case for an alternative belief system. However, the deeper he got into the data, the more apparent the mysteries, oddities and questions attached to the established theories, began to become obvious as parts of the equation, if the common denominator was accepted as this E.T. biogenetic creation thesis. They seemed to all mesh together as parts of a jigsaw puzzle, slowly beginning to make sense. He recalled how, at one point, he had reached for pen and paper and drew a long horizontal line across the length of a piece of A4. Under the line he wrote E.T. biogenetic creation, and along the top of the line he began to write the factors in, to complete the equation. He wrote; 'No conclusive fossil links. Evidence more akin to experimentation. Ancient and complete animal skeletons found. But no 'transitional' pre-human species. Longevity of alleged UFO phenomena, longevity of alleged human abductions. Analysis of human development by ongoing alleged abductions. DNA of human blood showing no connection with ancient apes and bipeds. Studies in mitochondrial DNA indicating recent origin for humankind.' He had quickly realized how many items, that were perplexing on their own, made sense when added to the equation.

In one of his paperbacks he had read about the theory of time dilation, where a long time would pass by on earth, but very little time would pass for the occupants of a star ship leaving earth and increasing its velocity towards the speed of light, and that any biogenetic engineering activity could be achieved between various visitations to earth, and manifest itself by fossil evidence appearing more like an experimentation programme than the ever scrutinizing and improving thesis preferred by Darwin. And sure, enough this is how it does appear in the fossil record.

Because of the obvious longevity of the UFO phenomenon that was apparent when one took all the historic references into account, it became obvious that the phenomenon was almost as old as writing itself, and that this should surely tell us something. To some, this longevity could suggest that the UFO phenomenon is just something that physicists do not yet understand. But such a conclusion would only hold good, if the phenomenon only manifested itself in plasma balls or dancing lights, but this was not the case. Many reputable people, sometimes well qualified, and others, considered as reliable witnesses, had reported actual close encounters with apparently structured aerial craft and sometimes their occupants. However, in spite of all these convincing cases, the possibility of misidentification and hallucination remained quite strong, and it was evident to anyone who made a study of the sightings through the ages, that the alleged craft were described according to the existing level of environment of that time. The phenomenon of alleged human abductions was part of the equation that John had included relative to their connection with this third alternative. And it was evident that the same longevity existed with regard to them also. One case emerged from the epic of Gilgamesh during the Sumerian era. The only possible conclusion John could come to with regard to ongoing abductions, was that if true, they could only represent a continual monitoring of human development and this clear interest in itself, implies perhaps, a certain 'responsibility' for human appearance in the first place. If the ET's forebears were responsible for human creation, then it would obviously be necessary for such an ongoing plan, to monitor the progress of the human creations, and in particular their mental development. An extraterrestrial intelligence discovering earth for the first time, could very soon satisfy their curiosity about human physiology by the abduction and analysis of the primary classifications of human racial types on earth, which would be the Asian, Caucasian and Negroid types. In other words, a maximum of only three human abductions. John began to be more intrigued than ever with this fantastic assumption as his list of contributory factors grew ever longer. He knew that Charles Darwin himself had waivered a little over the theory jointly arrived at by himself and Alfred Russell Wallace. Darwin decided to insert his escape clause and added "If the fossil links are not found then the theory falls down." As for A.R. Wallace, he departed from the theory altogether and John decided he had another factor to add to his equation. Using the words of A.R. Wallace himself and the stumbling block that prevented him from going along with it completely, as his contemporary continued to do so. A.R. Wallace wrestled with his 'unknown variable.' John added the words 'some unknown variable' to his ever-growing line of items above his common denominator. John had wondered at the time, how many items of circumstantial evidence would it take to bring him down off the fence? Which was the best approach? To accept a theory and cling to it at all costs, or sit on the fence of impartiality, forever waiting to be fully convinced with concrete evidence, that may never be forthcoming? John was aware of the philosophy of the ufologists and nothing could shake them.

Governmental bodies that were continually accused of covering up the facts were in a no-win situation. If they said nothing they had something to hide, if they stated that there was no evidence for an ET presence in earth space, the ufologists would simply react by stating "Well, that's what they would say, in order to save their embarrassment in having to admit they don't know how to deal with it."

As far as John was concerned, particularly with regard to their relevance to his own research and this third alternative, the issue was beyond the consideration that the UFO phenomenon indicated alien controlled structured craft operating in earth space, but the significance of their possible presence and their relevance if any to human   beginnings.   If they have been present throughout human history it would be easy to conclude that this was likely, but curious. ET's, discovering earth, after encountering so many barren worlds, would need a long period of time also, in which to study the enormous variety of earthly life forms, more specifically the dominant and in their view, perhaps the most dangerous of all the species, the human beings.

If it was known to any secret government agency that another world intelligence had actually altered human evolution, then this would be a much more compelling reason to maintain a cover up, than whether ET's did or did not exist in earth space. Even though, this in itself would be a fantastic enough revelation to the masses. People holding high political office and caring little other than the results of the next election, would see the phenomenon as political dynamite. And although being aware that the phenomenon was real and was indeed outsmarting their defense capabilities, would be terrified more by the thought of having to admit this to their voters, than anything else. However, responsible decisions may also result in the same situation, where a reticence to admit the phenomenon was real was being motivated by the possible results. Human hysteria and panic for example and the resultant casualties and damage that could all be avoided when a complete analysis of the problem may have shown little if any immediate threat to humanity, so why bother to tell them? John Willoughby, for his own part, was simply grateful, that he himself did not hold such a position, where clear headed sound judgment would be necessary. It would be easy to bow to the masses and get the millstone from around their necks once and for all. Otherwise it will simply continue forever. Or at least until such a hypothetical visiting intelligence decided themselves to reveal their presence. So why not risk the social disorientation and cultural shock and get it over with? After all, any kind of shock is ultimately healed by time and things would eventually return to some kind of normality. In all the cases John had studied, he hadn't found one that could point to direct aggression against humans. Pilots had been killed through enthusiasm and determination in chasing such objects through technical failure of their craft and were usually rewarded posthumously by being seen as having unsound judgment in chasing the planet Venus Menus or dying from 'anoxia.'

John concluded, that with regard to the sheer volume of unexplained events, or whether government bodies admit it or not, their defense forces were quite clearly being outsmarted by these objects. And this would apply to Great Britain Europe and the USA as well as a few other countries. But those countries with the properly equipped agencies and ability to study, compute and analyse the problem had surely by now, done so and brought to bear all their technology in an attempt to make some sense of it all, behind closed doors in some secretive computation process, while maintaining a front desk simply to put out standard policy on the issue. Although it was evident, at least publicly, that scientists in general, had avoided, side stepped, ignored or 'debunked' the phenomenon simply because it couldn't be tested and was therefore not worth pursuing. It was almost certain that government agencies had enlisted the help of science in their hypothetical analysis. Then at least, they would be getting paid for their efforts and would not need to struggle for some kind of government funding if they wished to study it openly and independently.

From what John had learned in his research, it was clear to him, that the so-called ufologists need not bother to accuse their various agencies (in the USA at least) that they had maintained a cover up, simply because, with regard to the freedom of information laws introduced in America, they have clearly demonstrated, that firstly there was a cover up, indicated by the volumes of data released, that they previously had denied they possessed, and secondly because of the heavily ruled out data in such documents obviously retained in uncensored original copies, they were still maintaining a cover up, protected by law and 'essential to the defense of the country,' etc., etc. Even presidents may not even be seen as having a "need to know.' They are only politicians after all, that come and go every few years. An agency that had maintained profound secrets for decades would not wish for such secrets to come out in some retired president's memoirs What then would this hypothetical super computer printout reveal? Clearly, if it was only a concentrated amount of convincing encounters that were fed in, then it could only indicate one of two things, either a natural phenomenon, (outside current scientific knowledge) or an actual extraterrestrial presence. However, the theory or possibility of extraterrestrial involvement in human evolution may pop up in the printout if the relevant factors were fed which would include any ancient E.T. visitations to earth and current alleged UFO encounters whose occupants could be the descendants of the beings who may have been the biogenetic 'creators.' The longevity of both alleged abductions and the UFO manifestations, the strange fossil record, the ancient legends all with a common theme, the only convincing 'ancestors' appearing 'suddenly' and already evolved and with no predecessor. The studies of human blood and mitochondrial DNA indicating a recent origin for humankind. Our inability to find the 'ancestors' years after the theory was set down and so forth. Of course, if the ufologists are correct in their assumption of a crash retrieval of a UFO and its occupants in the New Mexican desert, and this alleged event did actually occur, clearly there would be no need for such computer analysis in the first place. There would also be no need for a S.E.T.I. programme and all the expense of maintaining it either. Of course, with regard to the 'no win' situation governments are in, whether they like it or not, the ufologists view would be, that the authorities are happy to pay the price of S.E.T.I.

for no other reason than "if we are still looking, we can't have the evidence, can we?" John saw this as just another example of argument and counter-argument going nowhere but around in circles and this situation would prevail until the phenomenon was resolved one way or the other. John's two sons were quite interested, as were most boys their age, in the phenomenon and its possible implications and John had recalled watching a television programme with them regarding the so-called 'Roswell incident.' It was alleged to be based on fact and dealt with the subject of a crash retrieval supposedly of a UFO and its occupants near an Army Air base in the USA. It had been clearly alleged in the film that the death of the late U.S. defense secretary, James Forrestal, may not have been suicide after all but something far more sinister.

In the film, it was clear that what he and a certain group of others knew, should, according to Forrestal, be revealed to the population. And he wished for the contents of his diary (since gone missing) containing details of the event to be made public.

Apparently, Forrestal had visited the secret area, subsequently to become known as Area 51, where the retrieved ET craft and its occupants, one of whom was being kept alive, was situated. During the visit, certain telepathic dialogue ensued between the alien life form and Forrestal. The ET said more of them were coming to earth. But more importantly, as far as John was concerned, was the clear message in the film, that the alien's forebears had at some point in the past altered human evolution.

The rest of Forrestal's associates, who would eventually become known in ufological circles as 'The Majestic 12,' took a dim view of Forrestal's wish to go public and viewers were left with the clear implication, that they were involved in his ultimate demise.

Such profound knowledge by only a small group, retaining it for the fear of public reaction, would be quite believable, when they were aware of what had happened only a few years earlier when Orson Welles' realistic broadcast about Martian landings had caused widespread panic throughout the country. Their decision to withhold such information until a proper programme of lengthy preparation for cultural shock and social disorientation could be implemented, would be quite understandable. Even to the extent of the sacrificing of one person to avoid the many possible casualties that may have ensued if Forrestal had told all. After all a 'license to kill situation and political assassinations were more prevalent at one time earlier in the last century.

John saw this as just another piece of the mosaic with regard to this third alternative for human origins and there is no doubt that such revelations by any group knowing it to be true, that A.R.Wallace's 'unknown variable' was ET biogenetic creation, then there is no doubt that to release such information without adequate preparation would disturb many people indeed. It would also disturb historians, the religious and learning institutions and cause a massive discharge of assumptions, theories and beliefs, held hitherto for many generations, and John was quite convinced that if such knowledge was in the possession of a close knit group handed down to them from their predecessors, then it would be retained still, as no group would want the parcel to stop with them. Much easier to hand it down to their successors and let them deal with it.

John had considered how he himself would react if he were a member of such a group and what his own stance would be. And he could only conclude that (largely because of his profession), he would wish for it to become common knowledge, not only to allow the quest for human origins to be resolved once and for all, but that such profound information would eventually have to be released, and in that regard, the sooner it was done, the sooner the public could come to terms with it. Of course, John knew that the entire subject was little more than conjecture. Especially the convincing but nevertheless phony operations and post mortems on ET's alleged to have taken place, and films actually shown of them. It would be the most monumental event in history and reams of printed data on alien physiology, metabolism, cell structure, bone structure, DNA profiles microbiological factors, would fill volumes of printed textbooks and copies would be made and there would be no hope of keeping the entire mass of data free from prying eyes and something would be bound to emerge, on sale to the highest bidder on a secretive black market system, that had been secretly photographed and smuggled out from wherever it existed. In any case, convincing surgical operations had been shown as possible by horror film companies for decades.

However, John was sure of one thing. And that was, this third alternative's candidacy for A.R.Wallace's unknown variable was almost unassailable. But in spite of all the written data and assumptions, it was clear that no-one so far was able to offer any tangible proof or evidence for it other than the circumstantial kind.

Nevertheless, people who feel they are wise enough or qualified enough to write it off as nonsense should be aware that history is littered with pompous statements from apparently learned people, such as, "there are no stones in the sky, therefore stones cannot fall from the sky," and felt that their logic was unassailable at the time.

A certain author had once stated that if a scientist suggests a certain thing might be possible in the future, he was invariably correct. But if he states that a certain thing is impossible, he is almost certainly wrong.

Due no doubt in some measure, to the brandy he was consuming and the comfort of his study, a warm feeling was slowly coursing up from the depths of his being. John stretched out his legs and thought. "My God, when I think of all those rejection slips, I almost gave up." He felt that he should have known better than to offer his non-fiction work to the publishing houses that dealt with the mainstream academic and routine works of his profession, when it contained such radical material for mainstream anthropology to digest. But the fact was, the belief system did exist and did come under the subject of his profession and couldn't be written about in John's opinion, in any other way than an objective analysis of it, on what it had to offer, and this he felt he had achieved in *The Human Enigma.*

Many of his letters of support, convinced him that he had been right in risking personal derision in making it clear that other alternatives did exist alongside the Darwinian theory, and were open to anyone choosing to accept them and they ought to be respected if they could at least present some plausible data and evidence, even if it was purely circumstantial, and should not be derided by those who may be struggling to prove their own particular theory or belief with little success.

However, after all the interesting data and information had absorbed over the decades during his long interest in the subject of human origins and its associated mysteries and unaddressed questions, his logical processes, in the main, still tended toward the mainstream and scientifically acceptable view of his profession, namely the theory of primate ancestors. But it was the strange and unexplained burst of human development and rapid mental evolution that he chose to call 'supernatural' evolution that intrigued him the most. From the demise of the homo-erectus entity who still possessed an ape-like skull only 500 thousand years ago and who disappeared for no good reason; the human brain had amassed a further four or five hundred cc's of brain material which equates to an additional 100cc of material each hundred thousand years, when a fern leaf hadn't acquired even an extra leaf in 280 million years. But talking about 'large' brains was an irrelevance as far as John was concerned. It was the infusion of intelligent genes therein. Genes governing intelligence did exist and had now been identified and isolated. The Neanderthal's brain had been larger by a full 100cc's than modern man's but was obviously not endowed with sufficient intelligent genes. As genes are inherited, it would be logical to assume that if two exceptionally intelligent people married, their offspring should be highly intelligent. But it has not worked in practice, as an experiment. But in the natural course of events, it would occur anyway, with tutor's meetings at universities and so forth. Hereditary feeble-mindedness is a fact but may, as in the case of high intelligence, only manifest in other generations of the offspring still to come. Humans that appeared already evolved, that is, the upright artistic and creatively intelligent Cro-Magnon/Aurignacion peoples, who incidentally John saw as humanity's only convincing ancestor, certainly took some explaining, having no predecessor and this greatly developed brain that ensured its cultural evolution which began 40 thousand years ago, starting so soon after its possessor appeared, almost as though it was following a pre-ordained programme. The ancestors of modern humans replaced their unrelated predecessor almost immediately without laying a finger on them. There were no signs of conflict. The bones of Neanderthal had been found in stratified layers immediately below those of the Cro-Magnon peoples. Cro-Magnon came, the Neanderthals went, it was as simple as that. What was not so simple was the how? And why? Relative to it. John's eternal quest was to quantify or identify this 'exterior force' that brought about this rapid and advantageous mutational change when mutations for the most part were almost always disadvantageous and harmful in any species. It was quite evident in evolutionary processes in general that there was never any change for change's sake, in fact quite the opposite was the case. Flora and fauna remained each unto their kind for enormously long periods of time. Almost static genetic stability is evident when one considers that the primary classifications of marine life still evident today such as clams, starfish, shrimps, water fleas, sea lilies and brine, established themselves on earth half a billion years ago. The same incredibly long periods of genetic stability are also clearly evident in foliage, flies, fishes, spiders, crabs ants and insects in general, yet anatomically modem humans side step the entire process by amassing new brain tissue and bone structure as if other forces were also at work to duly shape shift and genetically change the human skull to its current shape, away from the sloping pithecoid form in order to accommodate this greatly advanced brain, particularly the forebrain the seat of the higher functions. There would of necessity with all this bone structural change going on, have to be major muscle re-routing and tissue building happening at the same time.

John could not accept that bipedalism was solely responsible for human development especially intelligence, as other creatures had also evolved bipedally with no obvious advantages. In any case a high-profile member of his profession across the Atlantic had stated, though not all his contemporaries agreed with him, that "bipedalism did not guarantee humans." The contention that exists and indeed had existed for decades within his profession became evident in an opposing statement that said, "without bipedalism our ancestors could not have become like us." With regard to his view that humans should be considered a separate genus from the strange Neanderthals and homo-erectus and especially the hominids, John took the view that they could simply be viewed as just another primate to join the 92 or so known varieties. It was certainly evident that in his opinion any such advantages over the true pongid apes they were alleged to have, were no advantage at all in helping to prevent their complete and utter demise, while the true apes all flourish and multiply and exist to this day without any such advantages. To John, it seemed quite obvious that if bipedalism could exist in a creature for 20 million years and after all that time it was still only using its upper limbs to tear into its prey, as was the case with Tyrannosaurus Rex, then bipedalism without any additional intelligence would be no advantage at all. And in this regard arms with manipulative fingers were entirely wasted on apes, when after their enormous primate evolution of 50 million years they still couldn't marriage even the simple task of peeling a banana, unless trained to do so, and to eat the fruit they simply split the pod and scoop it out.

John, like some of his colleagues that chose to admit it, was quite perplexed by the strange indications of the fossil record. It was necessary to depend on the accuracy of modem dating processes and of course to correctly identify the bone fossils in the first place. No gradually improving and slowly evolving process appears to be evident in the human bone fossil evidence at all. Even the small collection of hominid skulls seem more indicative of different species. And of course, he knew that no fossil links at all existed between the true pongid apes and the hominids and naturally, this would be the case if the hominids were, as he suspected, just another primate variety, in spite of their dentition or any other features for that matter. As for the date of that appearance of the 'pro-consul,' alleged to be the common ancestor of humans and modem apes, if indeed he had existed at all, was anyone's guess.

John was aware that those people involved in the ever-continuing search for the vital fossils, hated the term 'missing links' but missing they certainly were. Being open-minded and interested in the whole spectrum of origins. John had no problem in a visit to a natural history museum. But he had to conclude, that it must be rather frustrating for some of his colleagues to do so and view all those ancient dinosaur assemblies standing there with every bone in place, many revealed by natural erosion and not even searched for. Their bones were all at least 65 million years old, yet we struggle to find human remains from just a few million years ago. If that were not enough, the ones we do find only serve to perplex us and raise more questions. What was the anatomically modem skull deduced to be similar to modem man's and dated as 230 thousand years old, doing in that time period, when a more Pithecoid entity evident in the Neanderthal's appears some 100 thousand years after it?

John could sympathize with those people sweating it out 'in the field' so to speak and their efforts to make some sense of it all, as he had experienced it all himself. Many problems confront what some people call the 'stones and bones men,' and John admired their efforts and still retained the thought that eventually some conclusive proof will emerge to vindicate all their efforts. John himself had been involved in digs where apparent stone tools with evidence by microscopic analysis indicated their 'manufacture,' and that they were not natural stone flakes, but no bones had been found. Conversely bones had been found often enough with no stone tools evident. However, there were plenty of other archaeological digs going on all around the world and if no ancient cities are found there is at least a chance that as an interesting by-product, some ancient human remains may emerge from the diggings.

John was well aware that the paucity of bone fossil evidence relevant to Darwinian theory, ensures that even a small portion of an alleged ancient ancestral bone can cause worldwide headlines and the graphic artists are immediately commissioned to depict a human looking entity with just a hint of simian appearance, fully upright, spear in hand and in the pose of a noble hunter. The usual controversy then ensues, anthropologists in the main, act and have acted in the past, more in the manner of rivals than contemporaries when postulating on the significance of certain fossil discoveries, and contention disagreement and argument has always been a feature of their profession.

In the past, shortly after publication of Darwin's On Origins of The Species, there was an understandable compulsion to prove the theory as soon as possible and a new human genus was assumed from fossil finds, which were usually scraps, with almost monotonous regularity. In one case, from just a single tooth.

John sometimes wondered why he chose such a contentious profession. However, he had found the fieldwork interesting if a little frustrating, but his favourite work had been in the primate colonies. He was quite fond of animals in general which is why he found the letters from the animal rights extremists a little disturbing. They had misunderstood him and took the view that he was denigrating chimpanzees and their lack of intelligence when all he had set out to do was highlight the fact that time alone does little toward providing advanced traits, and in fact to identify the provider is by far the greatest challenge in the profession.

John's parents had originated in Ontario Canada, his grandfather, after distinguishing himself in the RAF towards the close of the second world war had brought his wife over from Canada and they settled happily in Britain. His grandfather had died relatively young, after taking early retirement from the aviation business. John believed his grandmother had been affected badly by his death as she appeared to lose interest in life and died herself shortly afterwards.

John often wondered if his long interest in the whole mystery of human beginnings stemmed from an incident in his youth. He had gone through the trauma of the examinations and found himself in a cloistered Catholic college before eventually going on to university. During his college days, where one addressed the sternly religious teachers as 'Brothers' he recalled an incident during an R.E. lesson where he had listened in wide eyed wonderment to the biblical story of Genesis and divine human creation. He remembered that he had caused an uneasy silence and apprehension throughout the classroom when he had raised his hand and asked in all innocence and seriousness "excuse me Brother Evans, if God always was, what do you think he was doing before he created everything?" Although he had asked the question in deadly seriousness, the outbursts of sniggering that erupted all around him after a period of silence, caused John to smile himself and this was immediately construed by the Brother, that John was trying to be funny or make a fool of him. The Brother picked up a piece of chalk and threw it as hard as he could at *him.* With eyes glaring he said, "you Willoughby, will stay behind after class and see me, now sit down."

During the rest of the lesson, that he only half listened to, John sat there brooding and suffering from a great sense of injustice. But he did hear the Brother emphasizing that they 'must all have faith and believe,' and so forth. John had noted how the Brother had looked pointedly at him when he related the story of doubting Thomas who refused to believe Christ had risen from the dead until he could see and feel the wounds. He had stared at John and said "I don't want any doubting Thomas's in my class. Right up to the point when he left college for university, John's nickname 'Tommo' had stuck with him. He was even called Tommo when meeting up with old college friends around his home town who all thought it was his real name and had long forgotten how he came by it. It was only after moving to the town where his wife was born that he finally shook it off. After his qualifications in zoology and anthropology, John had worked in museums of anthropology and primate colonies, both in the UK and abroad but his most interesting assignment was a position in a primate enclosure in south west England where visitors were allowed, after some coaching on monkey 'etiquette' to meet them. After a 'do and do not' briefing, the primates were allowed to intermingle with the visitors. It was quite interesting to watch the interaction between humans and the primate creatures as they weighed up their human visitors and their curiosity and intelligence though limited was obvious.

However, what did irritate him, in certain colonies mostly abroad, a compulsion seemed to exist among some of his contemporaries to enforce human attributes upon them. Apes were taught to chip stones together to get a sharp flake in order to cut the string on a box containing fruit, using the reward system. Mirrors were placed in cages to make them self-aware and every attempt was made to make them act in as human a way as possible. He knew of a much earlier experiment where chimpanzees were taken from birth and treated like human children with feeding bottles, nappies put on them and spoken to every day like a doting mother does to her human child. He thought, surely, they must have been aware that the chimpanzee, with its thorax high in the throat and its small undeveloped brain and total lack or 'brocas' area, said to govern speech, could never start saying 'mama' and comply with their request to become human-like. He saw the experiment as a complete waste of time and doomed to failure from the start. Earlier in his life, although retaining his Christian orientation and having a preference that every word in Genesis was true, John had found himself drifting away from doctrines that could only be supported with blind faith and consequently had leaned toward the more scientifically acceptable theories of a natural evolution from an ancient simian ancestor. He knew that the biblical version of human creation was regarded as mystic and unscientific by those without strong religious leanings and had to agree that certainly in the way it was written, it was comparatively easy for one to take that view.

For many people, it is very difficult to accept the notion of a divine infallible creator coming along and waving a majestic hand and having the whole process complete within seven days, when science has virtually proven the great span of time it took before humankind finally appeared on earth, not to mention the age of the universe itself, which is estimated to be somewhere between 15 and 20 billion years old. John could recall smiling along with the rest of the audience when watching the scene in the entertaining film 'Inherit the wind' where Spencer Tracy, playing a famous lawyer, virtually put the biblical writings of Genesis on trial as he verbally crucified the prosecutor William Bryan in the witness box. William Bryan had virtually turned the already outraged Tennessee townsfolk into a lynch mob against the schoolteacher John Scopes, who found himself in jail for teaching Darwinian evolution from "ape-like" ancestors to his class. William Bryan found his own strong beliefs on trial and was reduced to a mumbling incoherent by the skills of the defending lawyer.

Over the decades however, John Willoughby had slowly begun to realize that the theory of simian ancestry itself could now be put on trial with such paucity of hard fossil evidence to prove its case. He had kept his head down, like so many before him and hoped that eventually the vital fossil links will be discovered to finally prove it all.

Eventually, he began to feel like a fraud within his own profession, especially when he began to voice his concern and his articles began to appear in certain magazines and journals. The strange paradox existed, in that science, when regarding other theories for origins as 'mystic and unscientific,' finds scientific studies of the DNA of human blood and the analysis of mitochondrial DNA opposing the allegedly scientific theory of simian origins by indicating no connection with the ancient apes and bipeds but a comparatively recent origin for humankind.

Although frequent references are made to our ape-like 'ancestors' and out chimpanzee 'cousins' we are completely unable to construct any definite family tree back to any of the curious hominids who in spite of dentition or any other features could simply be viewed as just another primate variety of which today, some 90 or so varieties do exist.

As if to confirm the findings of the studies in mitochondrial DNA along comes our only convincing ancestor Cro-Magnon in fairly recent times already fully evolved bipedal and creatively and artistically orientated and quite intelligent. The more John studied the mysteries and strange anomalies pertaining to the theory supported by his chosen profession, the more he found himself becoming receptive and open minded to other theories on their merits and as a result he gradually became viewed as a radical or maverick within his own profession.

Nevertheless, he remained in his 'willing but not yet convinced' mode but certainly felt more willing than most of his colleagues to at least consider other theories on their merits and evidence (if any). Eventually, with all the doubts and uncertainty pertaining to the two major assumptions for human origins, he was receptive to any third alternative that may come along. And if it so qualified itself as at least worthy of consideration then he decided to carry out an impartial analysis of it. Now, it had, thus was born *The Human Enigma.*

In his book he made it clear to those who may be developing an interest in the mysterious subject of human origins, that no theory could be seen as written in stone or unassailable and no grounds existed for a slavish adherence to any of them and we may change our allegiance at any time, to any other theory if we so wished.

As John drained his glass, his warm comfortable feeling had slowly been replaced with one of apprehension and slight discomfort, even dread. He realized that in a very short time, the television programme dealing with, and exclusively based on his book, was about to begin. He began to feel like a Baron Frankenstein that had created a monster he could no longer control and that it was becoming a threat to him. He began to worry a little about the possible format of the programme. Although he had been to the studio, would the programme feature a panel of critical academics deriding his work? David Villiers had assured him it wouldn't happen, but maybe he was overruled. Although he tried to tell himself he was being irrational, he had already received quite a volume of correspondence from religious nuts and animal rights extremists. John was aware there had been a pre-programme advertisement or 'commercial.' His sons, though having seen it themselves, had not managed to record it. John had missed it himself. It may have been compiled at short notice; in any event, David Villiers had not told John about it. He was seen doing a street survey stopping and asking people about their origins. His sons laughingly told him about an incident where David had singled out a trio of youths and explained he was carrying out a survey on human origins and said to one of the youths "where do you think you come from?" the youth had replied "I know where I come from…. Balham." Then they all ran off laughing. David however, had apparently elicited some serious and intelligent replies and invited certain members of the public who seemed fairly neutral on the subject, yet interested, to partake in the select panel for the forthcoming programme.

Although John told himself he was foolishly overreacting by having thoughts of what the reaction of the public might be, perhaps it had already started. Both his sons were in their late teens yet still living at home and attending college. Both had related the odd story after the publicity generated by the publication of *The Human Enigma* had gathered momentum. His youngest son Bob told him that when he went into a fast food outlet, a group of friends came in behind him and one had whistled a few bars from the X-Files. Thomas related an event where a friend of his had made ape noises near him when approaching him from behind, all in a good-natured manner, but these events and his negative mail and the fact that so many people now knew where they lived worried him a little. He had discussed it with them and suggested moving nearer to the city Centre, away from this rather provincial neighbourhood. Although it received a rather lukewarm reception, particularly from his wife Carol, at least he had planted the thought for their consideration.

Three short raps on his study door told him that it was his oldest son Thomas, that was about to enter. He couldn't resist wanting to call him Thomas and his wife laughingly agreed when he had explained his reasons why.

Sure enough a close-cropped head appeared around the door. "Don't forget the programme Dad, it'll be on in half an hour." The head disappeared before John had a chance to answer. He went back to his reverie and reflected on the fact that he was a published author. Although it was a nice feeling, he didn't really consider himself an author, as such, but rather as someone who had written a book. His primary interest was the mystery of human origins. He couldn't imagine himself writing a crime thriller or a western, or 'whodunit' and certainly not a romantic novel.

Nevertheless, he had completed other manuscripts before the able assistance of David Villiers and now had other work to offer for consideration. He also had a six-month royalty cheque coming in, which in effect took more like eight months to actually arrive. And as well as certain income from earlier investments, was now comfortable enough financially to be able to concentrate on his writing.

John felt a certain Satisfaction in his assumption, that he had successfully conveyed the notion to the layman, that 'origins' still remain pretty much a mystery. And in spite of any pre-conceived notions due perhaps to subtle conditioning processes, all the facts were most certainly not in, and that any theory for how humans 'came to be' could be disputed or challenged.

A famous member of his profession had stated in his book that "No-one can stand up and declare this is how it happened." Although he was referring to the Darwinian concept John felt that this statement could apply to any of our current theories on the subject of origins.

John had often considered how disturbing Charles Darwin's revelations must have been to those people living some 140 years ago that were deeply religious, to be told that they were not created by the hand of God at all but stemmed from grunting ape-like creatures.

Surely to such people, this traumatic revelation would have been equal to that of people today being told that they were created genetically by beings from another world and having to come to terms with the cultural shock and social disorientation that would surely follow. However, those with little religious belief in the first place could surely have handled it without any problems. Even welcome it as it fitted in with other scientific revelations concerning the great age of the earth, and that it wasn't created in 4004 BC just after breakfast as stated by a certain Bishop Usher who had carried out certain calculations with regard to biblical events and reached this conclusion.

However, Charles Darwin became the 'New Messiah' and many flocked to his banner and must hope that they have not been led into a wilderness of doubt and uncertainty. But it certainly provided a more logical and scientifically acceptable alternative to doctrines only acceptable through blind faith.

John was well aware that science had been knocking on the church's door for centuries and some earlier astronomers such as Bruno had paid with their lives for such heretical revelations that earth was not the centre of all creation, John had read somewhere that Galileo had implored the church elders to 'at least look for yourselves,' as he tried to get them to look through the eyepiece of his telescope, in his attempt to explain his astronomical discoveries. John had considered the possibility that this constant barrage of scientific revelations could have brought about the downfall of the church completely, had it not been for widespread faith together with their thought that at least it hadn't yet been proven with regard to the fossil evidence that was expected to be found to back up Darwin's theories. Furthermore, archaeological discoveries had begun to make it clear, that the bible could not be simply written off as an unreliable source of data in its entirety. And so, many people kept their faith and continued to believe or sense a higher presence and did not regard the Darwinian argument as strong enough to divert them.

In spite of the disjointed and scrappy human fossil record, John accepted that evolution was struggling to produce the seemingly ideal body form with bipedal locomotion, and arms with manipulative fingers favourable for making things and this tendency appeared to manifest itself generally. But manipulative fingers were of little use to creatures without the necessary mental attributes in order to capitalize on them. One of John's major problems was to find an explanation as to how the human being could so defy the otherwise rigid laws of evolution and natural selection, by not only possessing this greatly over-endowed brain with even a large percentage of it still not utilized and presumably still to develop. Impartial evolution and natural selection has no favourites, and he could see no obvious reason why the naked ape should have been singled out for such favours, and if evolution was not responsible, who or what was? Many problems of a similar nature were in John's view, crying out for an adequate explanation and it was for this reason that he found his research for the alternative belief system that he called the third alternative, so interesting. The plain fact was, it did serve to provide some answers.

With his interest in astronomy and astrophysics he recalled finding it very easy to stay awake around 4am UK time to watch the first humans emerge onto the surface of the moon. Brought about largely due to the mastery of the brain's major endowment, a good capacity for mathematics. In mere thousands of years since the disappearance of the ape-skulled homo-erectus, humans had acquired this ability, when in 50 million years apes still totally lacked it. What then provided the human with this endowment? Although this lunar landing was described as the first giant leap for mankind it was of course the third such leap. The other two were mining out metallic ores and subsequently fashioning them into space craft. These major milestones in human history together with the capacity for mathematics, make it almost inevitable that mankind will journey, or could it perhaps be, return to the stars? It was only a question of time. John had concluded that when reviewing all these factors, the rather astounding conclusion could be, that some 'unknown variable' had purposely programmed humanity for this task or ultimate achievement. If it seemed unlikely that natural selection was responsible. Was it the intention of a divine infallible creator, that humans should go forth and multiply on other worlds? Perhaps ultimately to colonise the galaxy? After all, a 60-year search has failed to detect a peep out of any other cosmic intelligence unless of course they are already here, and some scientists postulate that humans could be the first multi-cellular reproducing intelligence.

John had little interest in science fiction, but he knew that it would tax the imaginative capabilities of even the most talented science fiction writer to postulate on what humans would be capable of in 50 million years' time, yet apes have already had this immense amount of evolution since the appearance of the earliest primates, yet their abilities and their brains remain small and undeveloped. Why then, after such an enormous evolution, do their simple activities astound some of his colleagues? And why can't they differentiate 'utilize' from 'make?' A chimp will strip the leaves off a twig and utilize it to poke an anthill and eat the insects. It hadn't made the twig. An amphibian will utilize a stone to crack open a shellfish when lying on its back in water. It hadn't made the stone. Birds will utilize gravity to achieve the same results by dropping a shellfish onto rocks. Humans utilize gravity to swing interplanetary probes around the solar system.

John found it rather sad to relate, that in spite of all the evolutionary effort to produce such a host of creatures, they are all doomed to ultimate destruction by the finite life of our star. Only the human with its so far unexplained endowments, has at least a chance to escape the ultimate end of the world. Unless of course, we choose to take some of them with us in some great departing Ark of the cosmos or at least their genetic material, and DNA profiles. John could well understand the motivation of some of his colleagues in the ape colonies who appeared to be trying to enforce human traits into the chimpanzees, as such a frustratingly small amount of fossil evidence existed. But he did not approve of subtle and devious methods to reinforce their view that chimps were our cousins, such as a ridiculous suggestion that chimps should be accorded 'human rights' as depicted in a past television programme. In spite of all their efforts in training the chimps or any other animal, one would never encounter an ape in the wild naturally making stone tools or encounter an elephant in the wild taking a bow or standing on one leg, or a horse among a wild herd stopping to entertain us with a dance, similar to an event in an equestrian show. Perhaps it was these types of comments that John had made in *The Human Enigma* that had caused him to receive all that negative correspondence. But in his opinion, they were simply facts and not derogatory to the animals, who after all, are only being exploited for human gain one way or the other, when trained to do such things, and even though they learn such clever tricks quite easily, they are never regarded as 'cousins!' Those who look for similarities to humans in apes, should remember the vast difference in genetic traits, which of course include the pelt, the barrel chest, the long arms and short legs. The incorrect hip joints, only suitable for knuckle walking on all fours. The different feet, hands with the different thumb, the skull, jaw, teeth, high thorax, with no chance of speech developing. And last of course, their tiny undeveloped brain. All of which are casually ignored in certain people's determination to see them as cousins, when they are nothing like humans at all.

John could recall watching the extreme intelligence of the dogs when on holiday in Wales and observing a sheep dog trial. The dogs had effectively and subtly imposed their canine will upon the flock by small and stealthy movements in various directions, and quietly conveyed their intention to the flock to do their bidding and enter the pens. He had tried to envisage how a chimp would do it. Its long arms in the air as it waddled toward the flock, lips curled back and shrieking, the flock would simply panic and stampede.

He had watched the amusing tea commercials and knew how much film lay on the cutting room floor as numerous takes were cobbled together to make the various mouth movements look like speech. He remembered the hapless TV personalities who had ignored the golden rule of not working with children or animals and then suffered some indignity such as having a wig pulled off after the chimp with its short attention span, lost interest and scampered off shrieking, and having to be brought under control by its keeper. Actors talked to chimps as though they understood every word, but after a wooden stare for a while they very quickly lost interest. John had written such things without any malice aforethought regarding the likeable chimps, who equally suffer as much indignity as they can cause, especially when dressed grotesquely in human clothes when being exploited for gain. John felt that it was the perpetrators of such acts that ought to have been on the receiving end of his negative correspondence and not himself.

With regard to the television programme he had observed, requesting human rights status for chimps, John had composed a letter to the producer, but later tore it up, that stated, "Perhaps we should confer human rights on pigs since their bodily material contributes so ably in human heart operations, or perhaps on parrots and mynah birds for imitating human speech so effectively, which is something chimps will probably never achieve."

John had been astounded to read of pigs being purposefully shot in Denmark after anesthetization in order to train N.A.T.O. army field surgeons in the removal of bullets. The reason given was because their physiology is so akin to humans. Perhaps we should search for a pig-like ancestor. John wondered what the animal rights people would do when learning of that little snippet. Although cows enjoyed already, a form of human rights in places such as India where people and traffic politely go around them or wait for them to move on, he could not envisage all the fences being taken down in Britain. In John's view a watchful eye should be kept on our current R.S.P.C.A. laws to ensure animals continued to be adequately cared for, but as for human rights being conferred on them on the one hand, and a whole industry being condoned and preserved to get some of them to our dinner tables to be eaten would be a strange paradox to endure, John had owned dogs in the past and could recall their bright intelligent gaze looking into his soul. He remembered how just a canine eyebrow would raise if he got up to make a cup of tea, but if he got up with the thought of taking it for a walk it would be jumping about with excitement long before he reached for the lead. Either the dog could tell the time, or it could read his mind, and as either assumption seemed most improbable he was left pondering the mysteries of canine perception.

Dogs were often cited as being able to detect psychic phenomena and even human mood changes. And even in one case, to the onset of an epileptic fit in its owner, and it would dutifully bark to warn her. Most useful in ensuring one was not handling boiling water or about to go up some stairs or climb a ladder. The amazing intelligence of other animals was largely ignored when focusing attention on alleged simian cousins such as the chimps.

When researching for the third section of his book he had read of secret experiments with dolphins and of naval experiments exploiting their high intelligence. He had found also, that attempts to learn their language of squeals, hoots and clicks in order to communicate with them for espionage purposes, had been made, perhaps to direct them to deposit mines under enemy ships. Since these events were occurring in the sixties perhaps there are those who can already speak fluent 'Dolphinese'.

John had pointed out in *The Human Enigma* that humans in general take their over- endowments for granted and rarely stop to reflect that almost everything we see around us was either built, laid out, planted, grown or cultivated by humans. One only has to pass an empty house perhaps once owned by a proud gardener, where now the house was gradually being swamped by the encroaching foliage, to imagine how the world would have looked after the demise of the dinosaurs and the re-emergence of all the foliage formerly stripped away as soon as it grew, by all those hungry mouths. The world would quickly return to this state again if there were no humans or no cattle to devour or cultivate it. When the primates established themselves on earth it would have been a true planet of the apes growing wild and uncultivated. The apes would have had no intellect or any kind of inclination to deal with it. In fact, they would have been delighted with it in order to hide from predators or simply climb above it.

John still couldn't shake his vague feeling of apprehension. They were going to talk about his book, his views; and people would assume all the data in the third alternative was from his own head. He wondered whether tomorrow morning, he would feel like stepping out of the door with pride or hiding himself away. He had been elated when his book was accepted for publication. The feeling was as good as he could imagine it to be in someone who had scooped the pools or won the lottery. However, it was not money or fame that he was really concerned about, it was just a simple wish to convey the message that human origins were still largely a complete mystery and that this factor should not be glossed over by assumption and conjecture but should be widely debated in an open forum and with regard to the latter at any rate, he had achieved his aim.

Now he had sown the wind and was about to reap the whirlwind. He hoped that the way he saw the third alternative presented to the TV audience in the studio would be received by the viewers as an impartial assessment of the data, facts and circumstantial evidence and not assumed to be his own radical notions. He had merely wished to convey the idea that if one wished to subscribe to this belief system, it seemed to have as much going for it as any other at the present time.

The E.T.H. or extra-terrestrial hypothesis and their possible involvement in human origins had certainly been well aired in the late 60's and 70's and all the data the viewers would be presented with came from this period, apart from any comments relative to the theory with regard to modern day advancements and discoveries. John was sure that even the substantial collection of books he had acquired was only a small proportion of those published on this topic. They seemed to be rolling off the presses with almost monotonous regularity in those times. Even in the 50's books dealing with flying saucers and their long golden-haired occupants appeared. These entities were usually interpreted as Venusians who all seemed to prefer talking to cafe owners or farm labourers, rather than heads of government when voicing their concerns over human behaviour patterns, and our more negative pursuits of exploding nuclear devices all over the world and ravaging our earthly environment to boot.

It was clear to John, that the people who made claims of close encounters such as these, were simply projecting their own fears and concerns into imaginary aliens to speak for them, as it seemed clear that no-one would listen to them personally. Today it seemed to be left to Greenpeace to speak for the rest of us and ironically to receive derision from all quarters for their efforts.

However, the deceit did not end with long-haired Venusians. Many fraudulent photographs were taken and were pondered over until the advent of more sophisticated photographic analysis techniques exposed them for what they were. Many a pie can or hubcap was hurled and photographed and many a model was suspended from cotton, of saucers hovering. And as long as a photographic expert stated the negative had not been tampered with, this was read as; the object was real. But people active in the search earlier in the century to prove the Darwinian concept were no less guilty of fraud. The outrageous Piltdown hoax of 1912 in Sussex remained undetected for some 40 years before modern methods of analysis detected it. It seems beyond belief how the perpetrators could have lived with themselves during such a lengthy period of time, knowing that many people must have been finally but reluctantly abandoning their former beliefs in the light of this convincing new 'evidence' that seemed to be the final proof of the 'apes to men' theory.

It appears that all the written data on the UFO phenomena of a few decades ago, followed the same pattern of preaching to the converted and trotting out the same convincing cases. Only a few looked beyond it and dealt with the possible psychological factors with regard to the observers and so forth. But it has become possible to consider, that it could be just a small part of a larger equation, with the common denominator being the subject of human origins itself. To be sure, whether his colleagues or any closed-minded scientists liked it or not, this so-called third alternative had now entered the frame and since it won't go away, in fact it appeared to be gathering momentum, then the sooner it was confronted and addressed, the better.

John had learned of a 600-page book that was known as the Condon Report, in which the entire E.T.H. or UFO phenomenon was written off as a natural phenomenon that our science does not yet understand, and that it was not worth pursuing. In other words, "we don't understand it, but further analysis would not help us to understand it," They thought it unlikely to advance the cause of science. Of course, the assumption exists that science is being highly advanced by deep analysis and 'back engineering' processes on captured alien craft in secret remote areas such as the oft quoted Area 51.

However, the Condon Report, which was designed to get the hot potatoes out of the lap of the Air Force and into the realms of science, the phenomenon refused to go away. If anything, reports tended to increase. John had read claims that professor Condon had been chosen because of his known sceptical view on the subject. Most scientists at the time were said to distance themselves from the topic and no doubt it in any case, saw little chance of any funding to study it, as the authorities were all too busy debunking it. Even today, study of the phenomenon is left to self-funded groups.

John knew the phenomenon and its hoaxers had now progressed from fraudulent photographs crop circles and a whole culture seems to be developing around them. He had read of two mature students, who in John's view would be better described as immature students, who had openly admitted producing some of them, and no doubt roared with laughter at all the conjecture about alien messages and so forth. John realized that people didn't really care about these amusing pranks, but he could see nothing amusing in the Piltdown fraud, if it did cause people to abandon their faith because of it. A human skull and brain capacity, with an ape-like jaw would seem to clinch the argument but it was an ape's jaw. It was outrageous enough in the trouble it caused the religious groups, but it also disturbed the paleo-anthropologists. Simply because these fossils were used as a kind of 'yardstick' in qualifying later discoveries, even causing them to be rejected as genuine ancestral fossils.

John was conversant with the data regarding the so-called 'Taung child' that the late Raymond Dart had claimed was on early pre-human ancestor in 1928. However, the controversy and dissenting opinion was just as strong within his profession then as it is today, and his contemporaries dismissed it as too young to be properly assessed, or that it was simply the distorted skull of a young chimpanzee. But more importantly, it was rejected when compared to the Piltdown finds that had not yet been revealed as a hoax and would remain undetected for another 25 years.

A couple of years ago, John had known that a television programme involving members of his profession was being produced and he had looked forward to seeing the completed series broadcast. He felt sure that the presenter who usually dealt with intellectual types of programmes, would ask a few pointed questions, but he was rather disappointed with it. When the presenter briefly broached the subject of human intelligence in comparison to the apes, he quickly retreated as the lady anthropologist began to relate her experience in her ape colony, where she imagined she bad observed a chimpanzee admiring the beauty of nature because it shambled down to the river, didn't eat or drink but simply stared then returned to where it came from. That very morning, John recalled that he had walked into another room, looked out of the window and thought, "now what the devil did I come in here for?" The harder he tried to remember, the less chance there seemed of it. Finally, he went back to where he started from and immediately remembered. His immediate conclusion was that if humans could be absent minded, who are light years ahead of apes in terms of intellect, then it's a pretty safe bet that apes will be also, this incident merely served to reinforce his belief that too much ape watching was producing too much conjecture on probably unspectacular ape behaviour.

He had often stated his position and attitude within his profession, which was "committed, but currently unconvinced" Most of those active within his profession would agree, that many more fossils of alleged ancient ancestors require to be discovered in order to produce a wider and more convincing picture regarding the whole theory of apes to men in all its detail. This certainly applied to the great biological transformation from true Pongid ape to a pre-human ancestor of which almost nothing is known.

However, John was ready for his full conversion on the road to such discoveries which could happen any time. Strangely, the forces of natural erosion seem reluctant to assist in the quest, when they do so quite readily with regard to dinosaur bones popping out of the ground here and there with almost monotonous regularity

As far as John Willoughby was concerned even the finding of a few complete skeletons of indisputable pre-human creatures, though helping to prove the theory, would not answer the questions regarding the supernatural evolution that was taking place in the later stages of the process, where the lightning development of the human brain with not only its' obvious over-endowments, but having additional cellular material in reserve, and presumably still to develop. We need to be able to satisfactorily explain the complete and utter disregard the human had in its development of the excruciatingly slow plodding evolutionary processors that do not change for changes sake and certainly do not allow any developments in advance of any creature's simple needs to survive on earth. Every time the problem is considered, it always begs the question, what was the 'unknown variable' or 'exterior force' that was brought to bear on the developing human, in the period of some (probably less than 100,000) years ago to produce an almost completely successful creature? Only the negative forces existing in the brain prevent the human from being seen as an evolutionary ideal or complete success.

John never felt that it was an exaggeration to say, that apes should be, not only teaching us in their universities, but have become masters of the universe after such an enormous evolution. Of course, he had to keep in mind, that the strange and rather purposeless dinosaur creatures were still just munching foliage for around four times as long the ape evolution, only to be immediately obliterated at the end. However, those prophets of doom continually worrying about extinction events on earth, ought to reflect on the fact that even if an asteroid did put paid to the dinosaurs, they were left alone for an incredibly long time of around 180 million years or more. At the rate of human technological advancement that prevails today, we ought to have enough time surely, to afford earth and ourselves the necessary protection, We can send space probes now to look over the larger asteroids, surely it's only a question of time before we put men in them, and perhaps a nuclear device or two, in order to direct them either into the sun or into Jupiter, which obliges even now by sweeping up some of the rubble that threatens us

John found himself jolted back to reality once more when he heard the front door open. He arose and left his study and found that it was his wife Carol. After an exchange of greetings, he asked her if she had eaten. "Yes," she replied, "I had a bite at Karen's…has it started yet?" "Just about to, I 'think," replied John. "Like a drink?" "Yes, I think so, a small sherry please." Carol stowed her coat away in a hall cupboard and disappeared into the lounge. John went back into his study and fixed Carol's drink. With all his reverie, he realised he hadn't eaten. He had read of people, usually scientists, getting so wrapped up in their problems and their work that they didn't eat properly. Although he didn't class himself as being on their level, he had simply forgotten to eat. He put down Carol's drink on a hall table and went into the kitchen. Shortly he returned with a cold sausage roll, picked up his wife's drink arid entered the lounge. When they were all positioned in their favourite chairs, Carol said, "couldn't you put that in the microwave?" Thomas, his oldest son said, "Dad has no respect for his digestive system." "Why should I have?" Said John grinning, "it had no respect for me last night." "Are you surprised, said Carol, "cheese and pickled gherkin before bed, I ask you!"

CHAPTER II

TRIAL BY TELEVISION

John Willoughby and his family made themselves comfortable as the familiar notes of the programme's haunting theme emanated from the television set. The title, *How did it happen?* appeared, then the graphics rolled prior to the start of the show.

This programme had gone off the air twice previously but always seemed to return to the screens. Possibly due to a combination of public demand and favourable ratings. It had become obvious to John, that many people were intrigued by the topics that appeared to disturb science a little, and quite often provoked derogatory remarks from them. It seemed easier to debunk or deride subjects like ghosts, UFOs, alleged abductions and paranormal phenomena, than make any serious attempt to investigate them, or offer anything in return to adequately explain them. No doubt, due to their inability to satisfactorily test or quantify these subjects it seemed easier to shun or debunk them. This certainly seemed to be the case regarding 'ooparts' or out of place artefacts that probably remain gathering dust in many a museum basement, unclassified and untouchable. John recalled reading a book that dealt with these items and it was stated that an employee of the Smithsonian Institute took a boatload of 'ooparts' out into the Atlantic and dumped them. John had decided that if this did really happen, then the perpetrators were displaying the same destructive ignorance as those who burned the priceless irreplaceable scrolls and knowledge from the Alexandrian Library in Egypt to heat the grand palace of the Conqueror after overrunning that land, and the destruction of ancient Mayan manuscripts after the Conquistadors' rampages in South America. The television viewers observed a Scene rather like a courtroom with rows of seated jurors, young and old, who had been invited to take part in the programme. They had been selected after articulate and intelligent reactions to a street survey, especially if they indicated an open-minded attitude to the question of human origins and showed some interest in the topic. Although they were in fact to act like a jury, their number was far more substantial. There must be, in John's estimation, at least forty people seated there. The view was changing and moving toward an open doorway where it then stopped. After a few seconds, a figure emerged from the doorway and took up a position standing in front of the seated audience. It was John's friend, David Villiers, barrister, politician and TV personality. He had a copy of a book held to his chest.

In one smooth movement, Tom, John's oldest son, left his seat and slid across the carpet on his knees like a footballer who was looking for praise after scoring a goal. Robert, John's other son, sniggered as Tom said, with his nose practically touching the TV screen, 'that's your book Dad." Then scampered back to his seat. John grinned to himself as his wife Carol snapped "I do wish you wouldn't do that."

When the camera showed a close up view of David Villiers, the title of John's book *The Human Enigma* was clearly visible. David began to speak. "Good evening to our viewers." Then turning his head to the seated audience, he added. "And good evening to our panel." He began walking slowly up and down in front of the bench and continued. "This programme tonight, is a specially extended production of *How did it Happen?* which of course, regular viewers will know, deals with unexplained and sometimes controversial phenomena; and attempts by analysis and discussion undertaken by guests considered proficient in their particular field, to formulate some sort of conclusion or answer to a certain subject. Usually we do not succeed but quite often some very interesting propositions, theories and suggestions emerge, as a result of our talking shop. This programme is only the first part of a two-part production; the second programme will feature an intense debate and assessment by those who express a wish to take part. More especially, those who are involved in the sciences that are attempting to settle the question of human origins. This programme however, will be based exclusively on the format of this book." Villiers held up the book. "By the author and anthropologist, John Willoughby" ..." In this book, the author lays out the facts, data, evidence whether circumstantial or otherwise, for three distinct belief systems as to how we humans 'came to be.' Why three belief systems? You may be asking yourselves. Well it used to be a straight fight. But, whereas the old and sometimes heated arguments may once have only been between the so-called evolutionists and creationists, the fact is, since those times a new and rather profound further theory has now entered the frame. A theory that at first, you may assume to be sheer science fiction. But if you have read this book, you will know, that it has in fact long been subscribed to by doctors, professors and even a NASA scientist, and a considerable amount of circumstantial evidence exists, that not only appears to support it, but clears up many of the anomalies that exist in the other, shall we say mainstream theories for our origins."

David Villiers moved to a kind of dais and placed John's book down among half a dozen or so other titles laying about on top of it. At the rear of the dais was a display screen rather like the weather forecasters use. A coiled flex with a push button fixture at its end, emanated from the side of the screen and was secured in a retaining clip.

David Villiers moved back in front of the audience to address them. "It has to be said, that John Willoughby's book *The Human Enigma*, has caused widespread debate not hitherto experienced in the media for generations. This didn't actually surprise the author, for that was precisely why he wrote it, he wished to promote such debate, on a subject that he sees as the greatest mystery of our time. To solve the mystery of our own human origins in all its intricacies is our greatest challenge. Our technological advancements are streaking ahead so rapidly that we may stand on the threshold of our final frontier, deep interstellar space. We seem then, to know where we are ultimately going but no-one can stand up and declare that they know where we came from. This programme is not expected to be able to do so. And I must stress, that it has neither the time nor the inclination to become entrapped tonight in complicated biological questions, gene patterns, or scientific data. That will occur in the second programme. And in that regard, any biologists, paleo-anthropologists or theologians and academic types who may wish to take part in such a programme in order to redress the balance so to speak, may phone, email or write to the special address to be flashed up at the end of this programme. We cannot really be fairer than that."

"As for this programme, it is meant to be a light-hearted approach to a nevertheless quite profound subject, how we humans came to be."

Villiers began to pace back and forth again in front of the audience. "Yours is an unenviable task, from your brief, you will know, that you were selected on our street survey largely because of your neutrality on the issue, or lack of pre-conceived notions or strong religious beliefs. This was necessary, in order for you to be as impartial as possible in your judgement or verdict that we hope you will be able to arrive at, by simple evaluation of the facts, evidence and data, presented to you, regarding three distinct belief systems held by most people, in the western world at any rate, for our presence on earth. If you feel you can produce a verdict, according to the evidence, which in your view seems the most logical explanation for human beginnings, then that is what we would like you to do."

"The author of the book on which this programme is based, although he is an anthropologist, does not consider himself chained slavishly to the entire Darwinian package. Possibly quite rare for someone in his profession. Others also agree that the theory as per Charles Darwin, has somehow turned into an unassailable dogma with far too many assumptions replacing hard fossil evidence which still continues to elude us in order to finally put the theory to bed, as it were. This view is certainly shared by more eminent members of his profession, who have stated that the evidence for this great biological transition from simian kind to homo-sapiens is scrappy and incomplete and that almost nothing is known of how the gap was bridged from the true Pongid apes, whose ancestry goes back to the earliest primates of 50 million years ago, to the appearance of an alleged ape-like pre-human. They have described the human bone fossil collection as a meagre fragmented array of isolated teeth and bones and portions of skulls. Other comments such as bipedalism did not guarantee humans, and anyone who thinks we have all the problems solved is surely deluding themselves, have all been made.

John Willoughby goes as far as to say, that almost as much blind faith that seem necessary to accept the writings of Genesis, viewed by science as mystic and unscientific, is also necessary in order to embrace the entire Darwinian package, and that many more bones, particularly complete skeletons of alleged human ancestors, are required in order to fully prove the theory beyond doubt. Most paleo-anthropologists will agree, that the ideal process, favoured by Charles Darwin, of evolution ever scrutinising, adding up all that is good and rejecting that which is bad, is not at all evident in the human fossil record, and that we are unable to trace our ancestry back to any viable family tree, to any of the strange hominids, which in any case all seem so Pithecoid in appearance. Some of their skulls have been cobbled together from many small fragments, up to 400 in one case, and finished off with plaster."

"You will also be presented with an equal amount of anomalies and questions with regard to human creation of the Genesis kind, subscribed to by countless people who have lived and died over the generations fully accepting it. They have kept their faith and retained their beliefs, not necessarily with blind faith, but because they have sensed a higher presence, and the Darwinian theory had not seemed strong enough to divert them."

"Finally, you will be presented with a rather substantial amount of circumstantial evidence, that appears to support a so-called 'third alternative.' That seriously suggests, that extra-terrestrial entities came to earth in our past and altered human evolution by biogenetic experimentation with a suitable primate. And propelled our evolution forward, particularly in our brain development, over a huge gulf of normal plodding and excruciatingly slow, natural evolutionary time. You may initially assume, that this theory is only subscribed to by those steeped in science fiction and *Star Trek* scenarios for years. But you would be wrong and may be in for a few surprises as to the amount of evidence, albeit circumstantial, that could be said to support this startling theory. We will begin our revue, by presenting the belief system relating to the story of Genesis."

Villiers went to the dais and picked up a mature copy of The Holy Bible. It was leather bound and showed signs of age. "This book, The Holy Bible, is published by the British and Foreign Bible Society. In the Old Testament, the story of Genesis is attributed entirely to Moses. In spite of the cold onslaught of science, its discoveries and its viewpoint that the story of divine human creation in Genesis is mystic and unscientific, many people have and still do, retain belief in it. One has to admit however, that in terms of cold logic, the creation of the entire universe including the solar system and all earthly creatures including ourselves, within 7 days can only be supported with blind faith."

"Of course, some theologians will attempt to explain these oddities with more acceptable logic or alternative meanings, such as days really mean 'eras' such as, for example, an older person may say to a younger, 'things were quite different in my day' clearly not referring to a period of 24 hours. Nevertheless, such eras would have to be particularly lengthy if our scientific calculations regarding the assumed age of our universe and solar system are correct. The Genesis story then, was written by a fallible man and not God himself. Students of theology will be well aware that there have been many versions of this book and even within a single text, there is evidence that many hands were at work. Furthermore, it is said, that the church leaders or popes, down through the ages, made many alterations to please various emperors and kings right up until the time of the intervention of the printing press, which virtually put a stop to it. It is said, that the bible did not establish itself into any coherent written form until about a thousand years after the destruction of the Temple by the Romans in Jerusalem in 70 A.D. The Old Testament is compiled from much older texts, with the New Testament being largely the Christian Bible and deals with the life of Jesus, the Acts of the Apostles, the Gospels and so forth. Can we assume then, that with all those alterations, it still retains its original stories and data? Even over just a few generations it has been shown that stories, legends, myths and traditions can be altered out of all proportion to their original form. This book is thousands of years old with regard to the data herein. Some might say yes, we can, simply because certain archaeological discoveries of fairly modem times have proven that this book cannot simply be disregarded as a valuable source of data. There is some truth in this, but some of the texts must be considered as unlikely to be in their original form."

"We will naturally be concentrating largely on the Old Testament and Genesis for the purpose of this programme, plus of course the events that followed it, and in the process looking at alternative ways of interpreting them in the light of our modern technological age."

"Strangely, the bible still retains the statement in the plural that says, 'let us make men in our image.' The words *us* and *our* imply a group of beings rather than an individual creator. It could also be argued, that the Genesis story is simply just another creation legend. After all, the basic theme is the same the world over. We could find little difference between a culture whose legends state, sky people came to earth and made men and the story of Genesis. Simply because (God and his Angels come from 'Heaven.' In other words, from somewhere other than earth, descended from our sky, set up a creation zone allegedly in Mesopotamia and stated, 'let us make men in our image.' "Every legend the world over, has God or lesser 'gods' making men. How do we explain this anomaly that appears to be a shared worldwide racial memory? Certain experiments with other living creatures have been carried out, that indicate memory can be inherited. How can so many legends from such widely separated groups, share the same general theme? Do we have to believe in this book implicitly or reject it? After all we can't pick out bits we like and accept them, and then reject other parts we are not so keen on. That would be like re-writing the bible to suit ourselves or our own preferences."

"It has to be said, that some of the events written about in the Old Testament could only be described as utterly fantastic, and if we accept them as true, then something very profound was occurring in those times on earth, particularly in the Middle Eastern zones and the lands of Egypt and Israel and the land known as Mesopotamia. A couple of decades ago, there was a trend for what we collectively term ancient astronauts. And many books appeared, that drew our attention to events in the ancient east. Certain writers began to single out events, in which biblical characters appeared to be witnessing some manifestation of an advanced technology, and strange aerial craft descending in front of them, and they struggled to describe what they had seen."

"The angels in the bible are rarely if ever described as we have come to imagine them from their image on our Christmas cards. The biblical angels ascended and descended on pillars of fire. How strange to think that during the Apollo programme, with all those lunar excursion modules ascending and descending on pillars of fire, that beings called angels were doing this on earth over 2,000 years ago. It must be agreed that with the hindsight afforded by our own modern advancement and technology, a startling alternative interpretation can easily be arrived at, regarding these events and activities on earth so long ago."

"In *The Human Enigma*, John Willoughby purposely introduced a third alternative for human origins. Primarily to prove that other alternatives were open to us, to subscribe to if we so wished. And this factor of apparently advanced technology in biblical times, in that context could be viewed as simply a small piece of a large jigsaw, relative to all that you will be attempting to decide this evening."

"We hope it is possible, through the medium of television, to deal with this subject of divine creation and the writings in this book, as respectfully as possible. We respect all forms of religion, and the beliefs of all those who retain their faith in the writings of this Holy Book. However, in dealing with this sensitive issue, it is necessary to ask questions… questions that cannot really be asked in any other way. And with regard to the aforementioned respect, we feel sure that any fair-minded person would also allow, that the same respect ought to be given to people whose views and beliefs differ from the writings presented herein."

"I would ask you to consider for example, how an atheistic person, who is surely entitled to his opinion that there is no God, would view the concept of a divine infallible being coming along, then by the wave of a Majestic hand, completes the business of creating the entire universe, including our solar system and all the creatures of earth including ourselves, within seven days, when cold impartial science tells us it took some 15-20 billion years from the event commonly known as the big bang to reach the point where humans finally appear on earth?"

"This fantastic explosive event, subscribed to by the astrophysicists, could be viewed as initial creation. Science has no really satisfactory answer as to how matter could come into being from nothing, and it could be argued that creation would seem to imply a creator. It is at this point that the scientific and theological viewpoints tend to merge. Where did the matter come from and what process caused the explosion? Was it a divine command? Let there be light would do very nicely. It would seem, to many people, that scientists must find a scientific explanation for everything. Some people have rather cynically remarked that they could find a formula to prove black was white if they had to. The scientific viewpoint is that time began with the universal big bang, and if God exists he was also created then. In other words, he is the universe. Otherwise, we would have to contemplate what would have occupied his time before the big bang; rather like eternity in reverse. Yet some religious teachings specify that God is, always was and always will be. Moreover, if science states time began with the universe, let us move back to a time period of say 20 billion years and five seconds. In five seconds time, the big bang will occur, it's only a matter of time… But wait a minute… If it's only a matter of time, then surely time did exist. If science tells us that black holes form by a massive star gravitationally collapsing in on itself until eventually even light cannot escape, then as that star was only a mere wisp of the material making up the entire universe, how on earth could the big bang possibly have occurred? Why did it not simply fall back in on itself to form a massive black hole or huge single star? However, there are more important questions for you to consider. For example, could a divine infallible God create such a disorderly universe? If other intelligent beings do exist in the universe, some must be experiencing indescribable horrors. Astrophysicists can detect colliding galaxies, great expanding gas clouds, unstable stars blowing up once in a while. Lethal radiation, comets, asteroids, meteors, all threatening any living beings or earth like worlds as well as our own with annihilation. He has also created erring, fallible and sometimes wicked and obviously faulty humans. Although this problem is sidestepped by certain teachings that state humans were purposely created with a proclivity for either good or bad deeds, and it is all down to ourselves to save ourselves or be damned, we must ask what would be the purpose of such an act? Especially since the Old Testament tells us that great annihilations of iniquitous cities and their occupants took place, and massive drowning in purposely organised floods wiped out all but a chosen few; then it would seem logical to conclude that if humans had been created purposely with faultiness built in so to speak, that they ought not to be punished for it."

"Some people might ask, if we detected a huge asteroid on a collision course with earth, would a wave of a majestic hand that created it in the first place, also get rid of it for us? One of the peculiarities of the human in our more negative pastimes, is the fact that the gross annual expenditure of most nations goes toward the procurement of bigger and better weaponry to annihilate each other, yet we spend not a penny piece to save the world from such celestial annihilation. Surely a curious thing?"

"However, if we confine our questions to divine human creation of the Genesis kind, it is fairly well known that science views the writings of Genesis as mystic and unscientific. To be sure, even theologians will be few in number who accept a seven-day event for the creation scenario, but some words in Genesis appear to be quite decidedly scientific. For example, Moses writes that the creator said, 'let the waters bring forth the moving creature that hath life.' In terms of earthly history, it is only comparatively recently that the consensus of opinion among science, agreed that lightning bolts stoked the primordial seas to produce the building blocks of life, in the form of amino acids, and reproduced it as an experiment in their laboratories. Where then did Moses obtain the information so long ago, that life began in the seas? We will come back to that question later."

"To return to the question of the floods and what sound rather like bombs raining down on those iniquitous inhabitants of Sodom and Gomorrah, clearly mistakes were made in the initial human creation programme. To save a small handful that would hopefully beget more of their kind, could quite logically be seen as a rather crude form of 'genetic cleansing.'

"We must also ask, since humans still annihilate each other in constant wars around the world, did the 'genetic cleansing' fail also? In spite of the amazing achievements and capabilities of the human brain at its best, we have a darker negative side that is evident in our more gross behaviour patterns. In fact, many would see the human entity as a product of a more fallible creator or creators than a divine infallible being."

"We struggle to produce evidence that the major Patriarchs even existed Egyptologists will point out that the Egyptian priests and scribes recorded everything, even what we might regard as trivia, such as the passing of migratory birds, yet fail to mention such a monumental event as Moses and the Exodus saga. The possibility exists however, that the scribes were expressly forbidden to even mention such a humiliating defeat of the pharaoh's army by mere slaves coming out of bondage and escaping scot free across the Red Sea after drowning an entire army. We know Rameses the second existed and most people know the story of the babe in the basket, who of course was Moses rescued from the Nile and brought up and educated on a par with the pharaoh himself. Is this how Moses came by his knowledge of how life began in the seas, informative wisdom from the Great Libraries? They were preserved and added to centuries later by the Greeks but burned wantonly to heat the palaces of subsequent conquerors. Of all the earthly creation legends, Genesis seems the most detailed and specific. What else could be seen as a more logical scientific process in the account? Why did there have to be a specific creation centre, protected by a fiery sword turning this way and that? Once more with the advent of laser technology we can put an alternative explanation on the revolving sword of fire, and a creator who simply waved a majestic hand to achieve his aims, would have no need for a creation centre, similarly, there would have been no need for the biological process or operation in order to produce Adam's wife Eve. Why not simply 'let Adam have a wife?' Why the surgical process of removing genetic material from Adam after inducing a deep sleep in him, or if you like, anaesthetising him? Moses tells us he was put to sleep, then incision made and afterwards closed up. It couldn't be clearer; a surgical operation took place. As for the process itself, once more modem technology affords us an answer, cloning pure and simple, where only the gender was changed to produce Eve. What of the entities accepted by the Patriarchs as angels? Fans of the James Bond films may have seen our hero strapping on a one-man jet pack and escaping from the villains over the rooftops, and perhaps not realising that it was a real person and a real piece of equipment, developed for the U.S. Marines. How profound it is, to stop and think that beings were doing just this in full view of the Patriarchs over two thousand years ago. Small wonder they fell on their faces in awe. It is fair and not facetious to ask why didn't angels descend on a pillar of fire in front of the late Mother Theresa, or perhaps today, in the Vatican gardens? Is it because they know that we have now developed the technology ourselves?"

"Those who take the trouble to read the Old Testament in detail as one would a book, will find many fantastic events occurring that puzzled the ancients but can be explained by modern day technology. In particular the method the angels employed to ascend and descend on their pillars of fire. If a U.S. marine descended with a strap-on jet pack in front of a tribe in the Amazonian interior, he would no doubt enter their legends as an angel. The strange paradox exists where angels led Moses and his escapees through the desert with the shaft of light beaming down from something above them to a mountain called Sinai, they received their human behavioural code, that is, The Commandments. One of the most important directives was, 'Thou shalt not kill,' yet the angels before a battle, actively directed Moses and his followers to kill all who opposed them. They were specifically directed to 'let not a creature that breathes, to live.' Moreover, in another battle, the angels annihilated 20,000 Assyrians themselves, and the Hebrews slept through the whole event. When they did finally awake, the Assyrians were all dead corpses. If we are told we must not take these stories regarding the angels too seriously, we must realise that many other biblical characters interacted with angels, which would make it difficult to take the entire Old Testament seriously."

"These questions always sound facetious but how can we ask them in any other way? There was a time when certain authors, even ourselves when asking these questions, would have been burned at the stake as heretics. Yet authors ask today 'was Jesus an astronaut? They ask, how else could a scenario be interpreted where beings from a place other than earth, Heaven if you like, descended and impregnated a chosen earthly female in a blinding light with a 'moving star' evident, and nine months later, a wonder child is born, who instructs his tutors, later walks on water, works miracles, cannot be killed by crucifixion, when others die easily on the cross, has his life functions restored by more beings of light then rises up to the same moving star that was present at the birth. Any light that moves about in the night sky, stops and starts cannot be anything other than a controlled aerial object. As we have already said, on close analysis of the angels and their earthly activities in the Old Testament, one quickly dispels the image of halos, wings and long white apparel. And we must also ask, where are the angels now? Although we have as much need of them today as the Patriarchs ever did, they are conspicuous by their absence. We must ask, is it because they never existed in the first place in spite of all the various events? Or is it because we today would put an entirely different interpretation on them?"

"The Old Testament contains amazing accounts of genetic implants and human procreative material removed and stored for later use." David Villiers opened the bible at a marked point. "Listen to this amazing account from 'Samuel 7 chapter 12' where King David is told; 'And when Thy days be fulfilled, and Thou sleep with Thy fathers, I will set up thy seed after Thee which shall proceed out of Thy bowels.' "This is a clear intention to remove and preserve and how else but by a form of refrigeration? reproductive material from King David for later use. A wise choice of donor, after all he did sire the wisest of kings, his own son Solomon."

Villiers flicked through the pages. "Confirmation is given in 'Luke 1. And I quote, 'Behold Thou shalt conceive in Thy womb and bring forth a son and the Lord God shall give unto him the throne of his father David,' unquote. Jesus was often referred to as 'Thou son of David.'

"The mother of the specially created being of great strength called Samson, was visited by a 'descending angel' who carried out the impregnation. Later they asked the angel its name. It replied, 'why do you ask this, when it is secret? Then roared up on a pillar of fire. Either these events really happened, or it is all a complete fabrication, there doesn't seem to be any middle ground. Modem life seems rather dull today, compared to what was happening over two thousand years ago in Mesopotamia. After this rather dramatic departure, Samson's parents to be, dutifully fell on their faces in awe, but what would they have seen if they had continued to watch the angel? What would it have roared up to? We know that above us is the atmosphere then interplanetary space. To the biblical characters 'above' meant Heaven. But the angel would have had to stop at some platform, structure or craft if you will, positioned somewhere above. It certainly must have been positioned higher than the craft in Jacob's close encounter, where he witnessed angels ascending and descending on a ladder and had no need for their jet packs."

"If these entities could and did frequently partake of earthly food and drink this should tell us something. It is extremely unlikely that divine angels would require food and drink. But whoever the entities were, they clearly saw no danger to themselves from the earthly microbes and bacteria in such earthly nourishment. Over the decades, various writers have suggested, that if these beings were not divine angels or figments of every biblical character's imagination, then the profound possibility exists, that they could be purposely bred alien hybrid beings and could comfortably operate in an earthly environment and be directed by more advanced and physiologically different beings."

"After an in-depth study of all the alleged abduction cases, they found that when hypnotic regression techniques were applied to the victims, they almost always referred to two different entities, namely, and in ufological parlance, the thin small and spindly greys and more human looking beings, working with them. For example, a well-known abduction case of a forestry worker in the USA, who awoke on the operating table and caused the greys to scamper away, then two human looking beings emerged to deal with him, the only difference was their golden hazel eyes. Did the victim encounter what the biblical characters would interpret as angels?"

"In the Old Testament, there is another amazing episode of an encounter of the very close kind with Jacob actually wrestling with an angel, As daybreak was approaching, the angel seemed concerned, and in any case seemed to have little physical strength, as Jacob got the better of it. But Jacob would not let go until the angel blessed him. It is apparent to those who study these texts, that there are many other characters mentioned in the Old Testament who must have been very special beings, as they could live for centuries. But there are strange paradoxes where certain beings have quite normal life spans while others such as Lamech, Noah's father, Methuselah and others lived for six or seven hundred years, while Abraham, for example only lived for a mere 175 years. Moses lists an enormous number of people, giving names, who they were and their huge life spans and so forth. What is it all about? What was going on in those times? Where was this creation centre where man was 'made?' A river is stated as flowing out of Eden and becoming four heads! One of them can be identified as it is clearly the Euphrates, but another is said to encompass the whole land of Ethiopia. So, Eden is situated anywhere between the Euphrates in a westerly direction across the Arabian peninsula and into East Africa. Was Moses being purposely vague?"

"One thing is clear and that is the appearance of Adam and Eve. Obviously, they were not ugly hominids or grotesque Neanderthals, they were reasonably attractive humans. Can this mean that human creation is a fairly recent event of only 50 to 100 thousand years ago? After all, the studies of mitochondrial DNA do indicate a fairly recent origin for humankind." "Who was the serpent-like entity mentioned in the Garden of Eden story? Were the created beings under some kind of test for their enquiring intelligence, their search for knowledge and their willpower? Although they were said to be cast out, the primary purpose of their creation was to 'subdue and replenish the earth.' If the earth was only recently created then we must ask, how was it that it was so neglected, and required subduing and replenishing? This suggests the creators arrived and encountered a mature but neglected world."

"Prior to the appearance of the anatomically modern Cro-Magnon people, the earth would have been replete with vegetation and fauna and a true planet of the apes but containing no creative intelligent species. We must also ask what racial characteristics did Adam and Eve possess? Would they have been the progenitors of three distinct earthly types; Negroid, Asian and Caucasian? How would that be possible?"

"When considering the bible as a whole, the most glaring paradox evident is the completely opposite policies of God the son to those of God the Father. In the New Testament we hear love thine enemies, forgive them, turn the other cheek. Gone are the hard-line policies of mass annihilation by floods and bombs, and turning even righteous people such as Lot's wife, to a pillar of salt for just looking. Gone also are the plagues, pestilences, boils and frogs and other human tribulations. We could ask, how would humanity fare with our constant wars and crime, if the hardliners return to power in Heaven today? Certain human behaviour still manifests evil."

"You may well ask, where is Heaven? Clearly it is not a place on earth. Is it just a state of mind and not a place at all? Can we be the only created entities in our backwoods area, orbiting a non-spectacular star in an equally non-spectacular galaxy when there are more stars, or if you like, suns in the heavens, than there are grains of sand on every beach on earth?

"Are there many different heavens to cater for all the other beings that surely must exist in all that multitude of stars? Surely, we could not all go to the same place. Can we believe in a heaven without also believing in a hell? Like black and no white, positive and no negative."

"To return to the biblical story of Exodus and the events during their desert campaigns. Moses clearly admits that in their battles, they not only killed every man, woman and child but their cattle as well. After all, the angels did say kill everything that breathes. Earlier, in Abraham's life and times, the angels themselves did the killing when they smote all those iniquitous humans, except in saving only a handful of righteous ones. Why were they told to avoid nearby cities and head for caves in the hills, was there a danger of fallout to nearby cities?"

"There is a much-quoted account concerning a biblical character called Ezekiel who apparently had a close encounter with a craft with eyes all around and wheels within wheels. Ezekiel took a full week to get over the shock of his close encounter as he dwelt by the River Chebar with certain people, 'astonished among them for seven days.' The more we analyse the activity of the angels, the easier it is to apply an alternative interpretation of their real identity. The angels were not all knowing, they needed to be informed. And they also needed to 'go down' and see for themselves. The obvious question is go down from 'what 'or' where?' clearly, they were in direct communication with their go-betweens the Patriarchs. Lot, Abraham's nephew, lived in the 'gate' of one of the cities earmarked for destruction; no doubt he informed Abraham who in turn informed the angels. When Abraham tried to bargain for the lives of any righteous ones in the city, the angels went down to some point out of town. They entered the town, had a good look around at what was going on, then departed and returned to wherever or whatever they came down from, and reported in some kind of aircrew debriefing process that they had observed no righteous beings. Clearly, we humans must be created in their image, if they could mingle so freely and unnoticed in the town. Two angels stood guard outside Lot's house the evening before the city was destroyed. A depraved mob came and wanted to know the angels, which in biblical parlance meant intimate relations, to put it mildly; the angels were well equipped to deal with them, and blinded the ringleaders of the mob. What with? Some kind of *Star Trek* phasers?"

"A common term of aliment in biblical times was to be stricken with the palsy, also there were many lepers. Could some of these people have been suffering from radiation burns or the effects of fallout? After all, Lot's family were advised to avoid nearby cities."

"In the story of the Tower of Babel, the angels again say, 'let us go down and investigate the matter. Would 'divine' angels need to go down and verify matters that their divine status should have allowed them to already be aware of? The plural arises again 'let us go down etc."

"With regard to Sodom and Gomorrah, Abraham stood watching from afar with the angels as their contemporaries were delivering the weapon on the unfortunate occupants and described it as one would when observing a distant explosion. 'All of a smoke, rising up as though from a furnace.' Was Abraham seeing a mushroom cloud from afar?

"The builders of the tower of Babel knew the angels were above them at some point in the sky and seemed to think that if they built their tower high enough they could reach their abode. The angels exercised some form of hypnotic mind control on them and caused them to become incoherent and speak in tongues."

'You have to keep in mind, that these angels were not from the imagination of one man or one particular event. They had clearly been on earth since they made men in their image and for centuries afterwards, and feature in the bible in events separated by many centuries. The quest would seem to be twofold. Did they actually exist on earth in those times, and what was their real identity? Divine angel or something else entirely? Where are they today? Where were they when six million people filed to their deaths during the Holocaust of the same religious persuasion of those they fed, watered and looked after so well after Exodus?" "What then were these amazing and profound events all about? Are we reading about the activities of those entities whose predecessors created men in their image?"

"The mission of Jesus was clearly as teacher and adviser in order to influence human behaviour patterns, but who really sent him? And where from? Heaven would seem to be more of a mental state, in other words a Utopian imaginary place such as Valhalla or a Happy Hunting Ground. Of course, if we accept the extraterrestrial hypothesis regarding the place of origin of the angels, could they be from the nearest sun-like star situated four and a half light years away? Jesus himself stated that his kingdom ' was not of this earth'. Although dwelling on the Old Testament in our quest for origins, we must briefly mention the New Testament and its admirable doctrines. This is not a book that instructs people to go out and kill anyone that speaks their mind and their own thoughts with regard to it, or suggests Jesus was an astronaut or tries to put an alternative interpretation on it. We are free to accept or reject it. Whatever we choose, the fact remains the teachings are faultless and admirable, and a clear recipe for peace and harmony on earth. The simplest analogies were used to convey very profound messages, in order to encourage the highest qualities of the human to emerge. It is clear that if everyone abided by these instructions and commandments, we would have no wars, mass slaughter of our fellow men, territorial disputes greed and racial intolerance."

"Although we struggle to find positive proof of the existence of Jesus and the Patriarchs, we do know that other people who lived, associated and interacted with them did historically exist, such as Pontius Pilate, and the Pharaoh Rameses the second, said to be the pharaoh whose army perished following his adversary Moses. The dead Sea Scrolls refer to a teacher of righteousness, although he is not specifically mentioned as Jesus."

"What did this man preach that warranted such a barbaric execution? He did not seem to involve himself in the political arena or challenge the puppet rulers of Rome. For all his fine words, the people of those times only saw fit to kill him." Villiers stared poignantly at the audience for a few seconds, then audibly snapped the bible shut and put it down on the dais. He continued "If the man Jesus was an emissary from somewhere other than earth we may call Heaven, then when he rose up to the same moving star that was also present at his birth, we must assume it was to go back there. As our frequent space activity has proven, rising up would eventually reach into space. So, we must assume something was waiting in the sky for Jesus, to receive him, after the completion of his mission on earth. Before his ascension he was revived (once more) involving beings of light and later, when he was received in the sky, would his mission be evaluated as at least partially successful? The answer must be yes. Simply because if other craft had continued in the observation mode in earth space, they would have observed many people dying at the hands of pagan Romans, rather than renouncing their beliefs."

"They would also observe more teachers of righteousness venturing into foreign lands, at no small risk to themselves, to preach the word. What greater thing can a man do other than lay down his life for a friend, his country or his beliefs? And so, as we terminate the data on this particular topic, it has probably become clear, that all these amazing events we can encounter, particular with regard to the Old Testament are not so much a question of belief or non-belief, but possibly more importantly they are a question of our correct interpretation of them. In either case, they seem to be inextricably linked with the entire unexplained mystery of human origins."

"Something quite profound had obviously occurred. To put it in. basic terms, humans were made in the image of the creator or creators. Tested for obedience and signs of intelligent enquiry. Told to 'go forth and multiply, subdue and replenish the earth.' Later they were found wanting with regard to their unacceptable behaviour patterns. Those whose gene patterns most resembled the creators by living for centuries are mentioned in a book that would still be read thousands of years later. Certain special beings such as Noah were selected and saved, others coldly terminated. Still the defective genes appeared. Entire cities and their occupants are obliterated. Eventually, a population distribution pattern begins. Though firmly directed by beings from a place other than earth, the credit and the blame for the killing and usurping of peoples from the various territories' rests with the human leader and his followers, and history records it all as human activity."

"Yet such victories as were achieved could not have been possible without the special equipment that was issued after explicit direction on the construction of same, by the mysterious ones. It caused enemies to drop dead by just handling it, or knocked huge city walls down flat, together with explicit instructions on destructive sound vibrations. How are all these events and more, connected to the whole question of human origins, where the creators seem to wield such power yet keep such a low profile themselves? How then, do we determine the identity of the creator or creators?"

"To sum up all the data then, what have we been talking about here? If we choose not to accept that it was a divine human creation by a divine infallible God and a host of angels, then what was it? And more importantly who were the angels? Are they still with us? If not, will they return? Alternative views could only be, that either it was all literary license, after all, it came entirely from the pens of just a few biblical characters whose very existence is questionable, or that it was a group of beings who treated humans very much like property, carried out genetic creation of certain humans to fulfil certain tasks, coldly carried out extermination programmes involving humans, and may have felt entirely at liberty to do so, they did indeed create humans in the first place."

"This strict code of behaviour that was handed out was observed by many, but also ignored by many, and wars killing, and heinous crimes continue to this day. The question must be, what do the yet to be determined creator or creators intend to do about it, and when?"

"Would it be a divine second coming with a host of angels, fully expected by certain religious groups, or something else entirely? Given the continual and questionable behaviour patterns evident in the human as well as our more positive attributes, it would seem, that a second coming was part of the plan in any case, as a divine creator, or a hypothetical group of creators, would be well aware that they hadn't quite got it right. Clearly the amazing events that are stated as having actually happened in the Old Testament make it equate to any good science fiction story ever written."

"But what we also have to consider is the aforementioned policy changes evident in the New Testament from the Old, when the wiping out of humans at a stroke was not given a second thought, but now however, the words are; 'forgive them,' 'love thine enemies,' turn the other cheek.' How do we explain such a contrasting change of policy? It implies an uncertainty and un-sureness on how to deal with the created beings of earth and the human question. But from where did the policy directive come? Long into the future, one could envisage such a complex; something like NASA, directing and controlling human cosmic explorers on far off worlds, should an amazing breakthrough ever occur in the means to achieve interstellar travel."

"Obviously, policy directives involving any advanced experimentation, or life-forms discovered, would come from the main complex on earth. Where then did the policy directives come from, that ordered the mass annihilation of faulty human creations? Was it from heaven or from another world?"

"It is strange that not one earthly legend states that the gods created creatures that later became men. Suddenly men were created as we are today, anatomically modern, and even more strangely, the scientific viewpoint admits to the perplexity of the Aurignacion/ Cro-Magnon Peoples appearing, with no predecessor, upright artistic intelligent and creative. What a strange meshing of completely opposite viewpoints regarding *The Human Enigma*, this really is."

"And so, to sum up, your task, as said, is to try and decide what have we been talking about here? Divine creation by an infallible, though entirely ruthless supreme God, or something else entirely?" Villiers picked up John's book again. "In this book, John Willoughby shows, that the entire range of fantastic events we have discussed in the Old Testament, could be inextricably linked, if we choose to view them in a certain way, and would tend, in that regard to be very supportive of the belief system called the third alternative, for human origins. But that is down to each individual's own personal interpretation of them. "Villiers moved to the table and took a drink of water from a decanter and glass provided, then returned to face the jurists. "Now, ladies and gentlemen, what of the theory widely taught, accepted and encouraged; that humans evolved from an ancient ape-like ancestor? Unless one has very strong religious convictions it would not be an alarming thought or proposition, even to those not entirely convinced that it is correct in every detail.

Modem theory has it, that both humans and modern apes stem from a common ancestor not yet discovered; and which could be described as the famous missing link. This creature has been named in advance of its discovery as the pro-consul. The sciences involved in the search, cannot agree on the supposed appearance of the pro-consul, if he appeared at all, and quote anything from 5 to 50 million years for its time period. If it was in the later time scale of 5 million years then surely there would be no need to produce more apes as well as the proto-humans, as the earth would have been replete with apes for millions of years already. What John Willoughby wanted to convey, was the fact that other alternatives are still open to us, and this is precisely the reason he wrote *The Human Enigma* in the first place. He feels that too much assumption and conjecture exist in place of the still undiscovered bone fossil evidence, in order to conclusively prove the theory beyond doubt, and that many problems bedevil a natural evolution from the primates. Indeed, he feels that almost as much blind faith as is needed to support the writings of Genesis, viewed by science as mystic and unscientific, is needed to support any assumption of a natural evolution from the primates. The Darwinian viewpoint of evolution, daily and hourly scrutinising, adding up all that is good, and rejecting that which is bad, is not at all reflected in the scrappy human fossil record, with its disjointed and strange anomalies of more modern skull portions preceding more Pithecoid fossils, such as the comparison with the Swanscombe skull, named after its area of discovery. These few scraps were deduced to be more anatomically modem than much later creatures, such as the Neanderthals. And so, you our panel will have much to digest tonight, with not only all the forthcoming data and anomalies in this theory, but also the factors relative to what John Willoughby calls the third alternative."

"However, it is now time to relate to you the data in regard to the Darwinian belief system, and a natural evolution from simian ancestors. There is a strange paradox in the scientific viewpoint that sees Genesis as mystic and unscientific and rejecting other theories that cannot be tested; yet almost to a man, they embraced a theory that when written, could not be tested at all, simply because not a single ancient fossil had been found. Darwin's contemporary, Alfred Russell Wallace diverted from the theory, simply because he could not accept a natural evolution, but felt some unknown variable was responsible, and quite evident in the later stages of human development in order to have produced the unique and greatly over-endowed human brain, that appeared to be developed so well in advance of its needs for the mere survival of the human on earth"

"This is particularly noticeable when considering the small brain of the ape, after its quite enormous evolutionary period, yet such creatures have proliferated and survived quite well without any such over-endowments evident in the human being." "The human intellectual capabilities in the best examples, utterly defy the theory of evolution and natural selection simply because these processes never over-endow any creature in advance of its needs to simply survive in an earthly environment." "Furthermore, the human brain has been provided with the amazing capacity for mathematical equation, which is totally unnecessary for mere survival, as is evident in other life-forms. The significance, to humans that is, of this capacity for mathematics will be further discussed when the data is presented to you for the so-called third alternative for human appearance." "However, suffice it to say, that the lightning development of the anatomically modern recent ancestors, known as Cro-Magnon or the Aurignacion type, requires to be more adequately addressed."

"The 'unknown variable,' that Darwin's contemporary A.R. Wallace tended toward, to explain these unique human qualities, that in modem parlance, put us light years ahead of any primate or alleged ape-like ancestor, was quite probably divine creation. And who is to stand up and say he was wrong? There are profound and very strong feelings in the human psyche that seem to sense a greater presence and no other theory they encounter, seems strong enough to divert them."

"However, together with our own rather fantastic technological achievements here on earth and the amazing achievements of genetic science and the future postulations in that field, we have to consider the possibility that during the enormous 180 million year dinosaur rule when no creative intelligence existed on earth, other extra-terrestrial races could have been achieving all the things we are only just discovering, and if they did discover earth long ago, then it is clear, that as well as divine creation considerations, for A.R. Wallace's unknown variable or exterior force being responsible for the profound over-endowments in the human brain, we do have a third alternative for you to consider when all the data for this belief system has been put to you. The primate ancestry is said to go back for some 50 million years, and there are some 90 or so current varieties, such as gorillas, chimps, baboons, spider monkeys, orang-utans, gibbons, tarsiers, lemurs, bush babies and so forth, and all their bones have been disappearing into the ground along with our own ancestors, for millennia."

"We have no fossil links to prove this amazing biological transition from true Pongid ape in ancient times. And as biologists are well aware, mutations are almost always harmful and detrimental to a species. Our immediate and only convincing ancestors are the Cro-Magnon or Aurignacion peoples that were just like ourselves and began their cultural evolution, being equipped with advanced intelligence, some 40 thousand years ago. They appeared fully evolved with no predecessor and swept away their Neanderthal predecessors, to whom they were not related; almost immediately, without laying a finger on them" Villiers picked up a bulky book.

"This book is packed with data regarding the strange Neanderthals, yet finally states 'they remain the subject of debate.' They seemed earmarked for oblivion, and it is said that later finds show them to be less advanced than earlier ones, indicating some form of retrogression was taking place, making them more ape-like, as though returning to their assumed pithecoid ancestry. It is said that certain studies of their bones revealed evidence of cannibalism among them. Yet others involved in the study of them say they appear to have attempted to bury their dead. In other words, a strange respect for them on the one hand, and a proclivity for eating them on the other."

"Their brains were actually larger than modern humans, once again highlighting the opposite ideal to the ever scrutinising and improving process that Charles Darwin preferred. Brain size, in any case seems irrelevant with regard to intellect and intelligence, especially when we consider the large elephant brain or the 22lb brain of the whale; or, at the other extreme, the intelligent activities of the ant."

"It is the infusion of intelligent genes in the neurons or brain cells, and the brain to body weight ratio, that seem to be the important factors when discussing brains. And so, the Neanderthals appeared to live a brute existence generally, and were not, it would appear, a human ancestor."

"With regard to the missing fossil links and the paucity of ancient human bone fossils in general, it may surprise some people to know that we don't possess a single skeleton, that could be described as 100% complete, of a really archaic ancestor, when it would seem that our natural History museums should be frill of them. The entire collection consists of a few partially complete skeletons, one the subject of dispute, and the other a Homo-Erectus entity."

"Homo-Erectus, as previously stated, still had an ape-like skull only 500 thousand years ago, and with the statements that the studies of the DNA or human blood, show no connection with the ancient apes and bipeds, and also the studies in mitochondrial DNA indicating a recent origin for humankind, people could be forgiven for assuming Homo- Erectus was just another, perhaps more advanced primate, to join the rather large array previously mentioned. Moreover, an eminent anthropologist from across the Atlantic stated in his work 'that bipedalism did not in any case guarantee humans.' How many people we wonder, are aware that when Charles Darwin made his breath-taking assumption that chimps and gorillas were man's closest living relatives, not a single ancient fossil of an archaic ancestor had been found. It was entirely theory."

"He did state however, that if the fossil links are not found then the theory falls down. Could people be blamed for asking is the theory falling down, since we are still engaged in the search for those vital links? Charles Darwin was nervous about the theory, being well aware of the effect it would have on religious beliefs. It was the more atheistic Thomas Huxley, who took up the cudgel to browbeat the quite understandably outraged ecclesiastics."

"An American author, in a work that looked closely at Darwin's life, stated that in the field of paleo-anthropological studies, he was an amateur, in that he did not teach in a university or work in a laboratory, but simply did science in his own home, without any trained staff and little fossil equipment. And of course, his contemporary Alfred Russell Wallace diverted from the theory completely. Charles Darwin also admitted in his written work, that with regard to certain problems regarding evolution, he had no immediate answer and that some people would experience a crowd of difficulties in accepting some of his statements."

"As well as missing fossil links in the later stages of the process, we also have missing fossil links in the ancient pre-Cambrian era of some five or six hundred million years ago. Vertebrates or marine creatures with skeletal frames appeared virtually from nowhere, in the aptly named Cambrian 'explosion' of life forms at that time, with only primitive jellyfish type of creatures preceding them. Charles Darwin could not account for it, and some 140 years later, neither can we."

"The oldest bacterial life forms in earth's most ancient rocks of over three billion years old, are the so-called blue/green algae, which it is postulated, could be used to commence the life process, or perhaps re-commence it on another planet such as Venus. Russian scientists have gone on record as saying Venus could be terraformed to a more reasonable environment in as little as 600 years. All this begs the question of course, which is; could the earth have itself been seeded as long ago by some fantastic process?"

"What then have we got so far? A theory by a man described as an amateur, who was a little nervous and unsure of it anyway, and whose contemporary diverted from it completely; with no ancient fossils yet found, and who stated 'if the fossil links are not found the theory falls down and nearly a century and a half later we are still searching for them"

"Anthropologists will generally agree, that the correct interpretation of old bones alleged to be human remains, has been, and still is, the most contentious by far, of all the sciences. In the early days of the theory, a new human genus was being proposed with almost monotonous regularity. Sometimes with just as little as a single tooth or scrap of bone. Almost every fragment, skull or almost complete skeleton has been the subject of contention and disagreement." "Enormous conjecture has resulted from the finding of a small scrap that sometimes resulted in a graphic portrayal of a noble looking human ancestor, with just faint traces of pithecoid appearance, spear in hand, hunting his prey."

"In the early days, shortly after the publication of Darwin's work, many people, probably lukewarm in any religious beliefs in any case, abandoned them in favour of this new and seemingly logical theory, but having so abandoned former beliefs, and as such having nowhere else to mm, it required the proving of the theory as quickly as possible, and the great quest for, and the analysis of, all the old bones they could find began."

"Even fraud was perpetrated by purposely burying human skull and ape jaw portions to be found in Piltdown, Sussex in 1912. This became known as the Piltdown Man and caused great excitement as a candidate for the vital missing link. This monumental deception not only disturbed many people attempting to retain their beliefs in divine creation, for forty long years, until it was discovered in the 'fifties, but disturbed the early paleo-anthropologists as well, simply because later finds were compared with this seemingly ideal fossil, such as Raymond Darts Taung child. To be explained later and viewed with suspicion as to being a likely ancestral entity. And so many people would have gone to their graves over the four decades that it remained undiscovered, filled with doubt and dismay regarding their faith, which had been shaken to its foundations. It was an outrageous act and could in fact, perhaps more successfully, be repeated again today."

"Let us look then, at the statements made by certain anthropologists today, some 140 years after the publication of Darwin's breathless and quite daring assumption that chimpanzees and gorillas were man's closest living relatives, with not a particle of evidence in hand to sustain it." Villiers picked up a few small sheets of paper and placed them back on the dais as he read them out. "Our current fossil collection is a mere fragmented array of isolated teeth and bones and portions of skulls; the evidence is scrappy and incomplete. So many family trees exist, that it is hard to see the trees for the forest.'...

"It is the dream of every anthropologist to discover a complete skeleton of an archaic ancestor... 'Bipedalism did not guarantee humans.'.... 'Anyone who thinks we have all the answers is surely deluding themselves.'...'No-one can stand up and declare that they know how it happened. They also speak of the folly of a slavish adherence to the entire Darwinian package."

"Yet for all these rather negative comments, the view is still maintained and projected that the theory is totally unassailable. The plain fact is, the layman or average man in the street will not encounter, or at least did not encounter, until the recent publication of *The Human Enigma*, any reference to such comments on television or radio programmes. They are only to be found in anthropological and natural history works on human evolution, available in most good libraries, but only if one chooses to analyse the evidence for oneself, which of course, most people do not. Consequently, they naturally assume when constantly hearing about chimp cousins and ape-like ancestors, that all the facts are in."

"They may have watched a recent television programme that allowed anthropologists to seriously ask for human rights for chimpanzees. They may also assume that seriously exploited chimpanzees, dressed grotesquely in human clothes for a tea commercial, really are speaking. They may also see chimps doing things they have been trained industriously to do, and consider they are acting naturally. Such as chipping stones together to get a sharp flake of stone to cut the strings on a box containing fruit, utilising the reward system, or performing other clever tricks. John Willoughby's advice to such people is to visit the wild habitats of any creature and see if they can f i n d a chimp stone tools, an elephant standing on one leg or taking a bow, a wild horse prancing like those in an equestrian show, a seal balancing a ball on its nose, or a dog herding sheep without being trained to do so."

"Does it not seem strange; that we have an abundance of old bones in order to construct complete 65-million-year-old skeletons quite often discovered due to natural erosion when we cannot muster a single skeleton of an agreed and indisputable ancient human ancestor to stand alongside them?"

"We have a substantial collection of old but anatomically modern Cro-Magnon bones and an abundance of Neanderthal fossils, but really ancient ancestors are another matter. The so-called Turkana Boy is almost complete, but it is a Homo-Erectus entity and therefore possessed an ape-like skull. And the creature christened Lucy, alleged to be an Australoperine ancestor is only 40% complete with many ape-like features, and is the subject of the usual contention and disagreement, even the sex of the creature has not been agreed upon."

"Why then can't we find the old bones to put Darwin's theory to bed, when we continually stumble over ancient dinosaur bones without even looking for them?"

"In 1928 Raymond Dart's Taung baby was dismissed by his contemporaries as simply the distorted skull of a young chimpanzee and was viewed with suspicion when compared with the ideal find of the Piltdown Man, only to be discovered as a fraud some '25 years later."

"It does seem strange that where the processes of natural erosion quite often oblige by uncovering old dinosaur bones quite regularly, they singularly fail to do so with regard to ancient human remains. No doubt the enormous conjecture made, regarding the significance of any item found and classified by the so-called bones and stones men, is due in some small measure, to this frustrating inability to make a positive and profound discovery. For example, a recent television programme depicted a find in Australia as a manufactured stone tool. Immediately the conjecture began, that attempted to raise the stature of Homo Habilis, or man the toolmaker, an entity of itself conjectured from a few small scraps; to an expert navigator, explorer and boat builder, with the intelligence to cross the Pacific and take up residence in Australia and begin fashioning stone tools. All this without a scrap of bone in sight."

"Similarly, with regard to Neanderthal man, strenuous attempts are frequently made to raise their cultural status from a brute existence. For example, a neatly broken arm bone, found on a creature whose genus already exhibits congenital bone deformities and a form of evolutionary retrogression, becomes a skilful surgical amputation carried out by a Neanderthal surgeon."

'The anthropologist F. Clerk Howell points out that Neanderthals exhibited puzzling evolutionary tendencies by becoming more primitive, not less so and the fossils more recently discovered of them, indicate creatures even bulkier, squatter and more beetle- browed than their predecessors."

"John Willoughby feels that Homo-Sapiens, that is ourselves, ushered in with the arrival of Cro-Magnon men or the Aurignacion type, should not be classified in the Homo genus along with the Neanderthal and Homo Erectus, but ought to qualify as a separate entity altogether, that is the distinct genus Homo Sapiens - Sapiens. His major qualification for this status being the amazing and incomparable brain and the distinct absence of a predecessor."

"If, as is evident, when we set out on the road of discovery, we cannot get past the Neanderthals, who were unrelated and non-interbreeding with the Cro-Magnon peoples, there is little hope of any family tree reaching back in any convincing manner to the owners of the rather grotesque hominid skulls. In spite of any special features, dentition and so forth, the robust and more gracile both display distinctly simian characteristics and do not appear to be on a direct line of descent to modem humans. Anthropologist's themselves have suggested that they appear more as different species rather than anything depicting a gradually improving process. The skulls of the robust Australopithecines with their sagittal crests and lowering brow ridges, seem little different from a type of gorilla."

David Villiers walked to the screen and took the cable with the press button fitting and lit up the screen. A series of large grotesque skulls filled the screen intermittently, as he pressed the button. "There is certainly no sign here of Charles Darwin's evolutionary process, daily and hourly scrutinising, rejecting that which is bad and adding up and preserving all that is good." If these creatures could be brought back to life in some futuristic Jurassic Park experiment, we would struggle to see any human traits in their body form." Villiers pressed the button again and a small partially formed skeleton was shown. "This is the 40% complete skeleton of a small Australopithecine christened 'Lucy' alleged to be an upright ancient ancestor. But it has many ape-like features and has curved finger and toe bones, and walking upright would have been rather difficult, if not painful for her. With the conjecture and dissent always evident in this contentious science, the creature's gender is now under reconsideration."

Villiers pressed the button again. "This is an almost complete skeleton of a young Homo- Erectus entity called the Turkana Boy. The term boy may seem to be questionable in a creature such as this, with its ape-like skull, but with 8-900cc of brain material, it certainly had a larger brain than our alleged chimpanzee cousins, but in order to transform into a human, it had a mammoth task to pull off in natural evolution, so evident with all that genetic stability in everything else, in order to increase its brain material by another 500cc's. Yet this is precisely what happened in mere thousands of years for such a slow process to suddenly produce the human. This of course assumes that Homo-Erectus was a human ancestor, for which there is no indisputable evidence. If humans were not related to Neanderthal, how could we be related to Homo-Erectus, a predecessor of Neanderthal?" Villiers flicked the image off and went back to Lucy. "If we return again to this creature called Lucy, a nickname given at the time of its discovery, because a   Beatles' song   Lucy in the Sky with Diamonds happened to be popular at that time. We must consider it to be the oldest alleged ancestor as it is estimated to be some 3 million years old. Some tracks were found near the zone of its discovery now known as the Laetoli tracks made in volcanic ash, solidified with age and dated from a similar time period. They appear to show upright walkers were around at the time. With the usual contention ever present, it was stated that Lucy did not make the tracks with its curved toe bones, and that on top of this, Lucy may be a "he".

"As well as the aforementioned curved finger and toe bones, it has long arms, short legs, a barrel chest and an ape-like skull. Were there really bipedal upright walkers 3 million years ago? Can we really trust our dating processes?" Villiers switched off the screen and walked to the dais.

I have here, a dating anomaly highlighted by a Soviet scientist E.K. Gerling who analysed rock formations from deep beneath the Baltic Crust. The accepted age of the earth is usually agreed to be dated as four and a half billion years old, but the Soviet scientist obtained consistent readings of six and a half billion years. This date was arrived at by measuring radioactive Potassium 40 as it changed to Argon 40. This system of dating is often used by our own scientists. We must also ask, with regard to the array of hominid skulls, made up, in one case from 400 separate pieces; was each piece painstakingly dated and identified as coming from the same time period and belonging to the same skull?"

"The skeleton of the so-called Turkana Boy shown a moment ago, was put together from pieces found during five seasons in the field, stretching over more than seven months and involving the removal of fifteen hundred tons of sediment. Can we be assured that every single piece was accurately tested and dated and definitely belonged to the same creature? In the words of a famous anthropologist. "There are many traps for the unwary". It is often stated that the bones of many other creatures are usually found with the alleged human ancestral remains. There must be a great potential for error."

"We could picture a scenario for example, of a habitat or a cave, where bones were found, that could have been occupied by ancestors, then animals, then apes, then back to ancestors again over long time periods; and all this great admixture of bones, which would also include food waste from predators, all disappearing into the ground and having similar ages when finally discovered many thousands, perhaps millions of years later."

'no-one would wish to detract from the ability of the paleo-anthropologists to correctly identify old bones, but the British Museum Press certainly agrees that there is great potential for error.' Villiers picked up another written quote from the dais.

"This is from their paper of 1994 regarding a title, Human Remains, and I quote... 'Isolated fragments of bones and teeth can easily be misidentified. Fragmentary human bones are sometimes being confused with those of large carnivores such as bears. ... fragments of the limb bones of large birds such as swans or geese are also mistaken for human remains.' End of quote." "So...we must conclude that the eminent anthropologist was correct when he said there are many traps for the unwary.' With regard to these quotations I am pointing out to you, copies of them are placed in front of you on the ledges when you retire to consider a verdict, please take them with you." "With regard to dating anomalies, there are other instances where our scientific, and assumed to be reliable, dating processes, might be viewed as suspect."

Villiers picked up yet another piece of paper. This is from a work dealing with lunar mysteries and anomalies that stemmed from the Apollo programme and the retrieval of moon rocks and the subsequent dating thereof. The quote begins, "it should be noted, that NASA officially recognises the oldest rock to be 4.5 billion years old, but there are however, other reports. According to Sky and Telescope, a well-known astronomical periodical, the lunar conference that followed the final Apollo mission revealed that a moon rock was dated at 5.3 billion years old." Villiers broke off from the quote and looked directly at the panel. "Older than our solar system, ladies and gentlemen. To continue .... Another report based on the potassium" argon system of dating, accepted by and frequently used by science as an accurate dating system, claimed that some rocks give an unacceptable age of seven billion years. And if we are to believe yet another report, 'two Apollo 12 rocks have been dated as 20 billion years old,' end of quote. This is all really quite astounding ladies and gentlemen. It is amazing enough for moon rocks to be older than the computed age of our solar system. But to be older than creation itself, or our alleged 'big bang' clearly, something is going very wrong somewhere. Astrophysicists used to generally agree, that the universe was 15 to 20 billion years old, but the figure has now been revised downwards and we hear 12 billion years frequently quoted."

"And so, you can see ladies and gentlemen, although the predominant scientific view is that the story in Genesis for human origins is mystic and unscientific, and the third alternative was not even discussed until publication of *The Human Enigma*, they have many mysteries and anomalies to address in the theory of Darwinian evolution itself."

Although we are often treated to animated films and depictions of a sort of lungfish slithering out of the primordial seas away from all the marine predators that would devour it, then having its fins evolve into legs, becoming lizards, crocodiles, then rearing up on two legs and going through a whole series of changing species, finally to primates and upright humans. Producing the skeletal remains is quite a different proposition.

Species are prevented from cross-breeding and remain 'each unto their kind' as the bible states, because their chromosome pattern is different in each species. "Man/apes could never be produced by inseminating our alleged cousins with human genetic reproductive material because of this rigid genetic pattern arrangement. If it was possible there would be chaos among life forms on earth. How then did the evolutionary processes so casually defy such rigid laws, that life forms are subject to today? No natural history museum anywhere in the world can produce a transitional skeletal form of one creature changing into another species."

"Clearly, the grand leap from simian to 'homo' could have required a major advantageous mutational change. The general theory of evolution is based on the premise of the culmination of small favourable gene mutations, but geneticists will generally agree, that in more than 99% of cases the mutation of a gene produces some kind of harmful effect or some disturbance of function, and in any case, natural gene mutations have proved to be so infrequent that the genes of earthly living things and their hereditary characteristics, have been calculated to remain stable for millions of years."

"Many species of plant and animal life are basically identical to their fossil ancestors of nearly half a billion years ago. We have on earth, experienced the two major factors causing gene disruption, and they are radiation and its adverse effects and chemicals such as the drug Thalidomide, that had such devastating effects on new born children decades ago."

"The point that emerges here is, the major and quite apparent genetic stability that exists on earth in all forms of life. Of course, there has been change within kind, for adaptability and so forth, and a good example is the horse, which has developed from its original size, which was only a little larger than a good-sized dog. Mankind was rather fortunate with this coincidental enlargement of a creature that would ultimately assist him greatly with his farming and transport problems; and when we deal with the third alternative for human origins, you may like to consider the possibility that the unknown variable, or exterior force that A.R. Wallace wrestled with, and that we will be considering for the rapid development of the human in the later stages of evolution, may also have been applied to the horse."

"Is it really so surprising that A.R. Wallace voiced such perplexity over the unique human, and its mental over-endowments that so utterly defy the evolutionary and natural selection processes, that have no favourites, and never over-endow any creature in advance of its simple needs for survival?"

"What is so surprising, is that many people involved in the quest for the missing links, assume without question that the human is simply a naked ape, and his amazing mental over-endowments are a natural bequest from a simian ancestor. When apes themselves are completely devoid of creative intelligence, other than relative to simple survival needs, when they have had some 50 million years of evolution from the earliest primates to achieve it."

"The most imaginative science fiction writer would be hard pressed to assume what humans might be achieving, when booking at the explosive advancements currently occurring in the sciences if we still exist after such a period of time." "Anthropologists will generally agree, that many more ancient skeletons, preferably complete, will have to be discovered in order to complete the picture and truly show how this great and rather miraculous biological transformation from ape-hood to humans actually occurred. It would be interesting to consider what Darwin's viewpoint would be today, if he could somehow come amongst us. After all it is now 150 years since he stated, 'If the fossil links are not found then the theory falls down.' And we are no nearer to solving all the problems with our scrappy fossil array, than when Darwin was alive."

"We seem unable to get past the first predecessor of our immediate and anatomically modern ancestor, the Cro-Magnon people. They were not related to the Neanderthals, so how can we go about the process of constructing any viable family tree back to the rather pithecoid, not to say grotesque Hominids, represented by a half a dozen or so skulls?"

"Even with the few examples we have, they have been cobbled together from as many as 400 pieces and have been completed in their assumed form by a heavy reliance on plaster. One might assume that the ideal scenario would be, a sudden prolific volume of numerous skeletons being found, in some preserving clay seam for example, that not only had the lower jaw and cranium intact, but the pelvic and hip joint areas also complete. And if we could make two or three such discoveries, from widely differing periods into the past, then we could observe the gradually evolving human slowly discarding his simian traits."

"However, this situation seems most unlikely, but why, when we can so successfully construct such a volume of ancient animal bones, evident in the dinosaurs, now in our museums? If we only found a few skulls that were obviously on a direct line of descent to humans and could observe the foramen magnum or point of entry of the spinal column into the skull, then it would become clear, even without the discovery of the pelvic bones, that if this point of entry was seen to be moving forward and was evident in the later finds, then upright stance could at least be seen to be occurring, but even then, when an anthropologist from across the Atlantic stated Bipedalism did not guarantee humans' we still have problems. Why couldn't there have been upright apes? After all, the Tyrannosaurus Rex was an upright walker and that creature was said to have lasted for 20 million years. Yet, in all that immense period of time, his bipedalism counted for nothing. Was Homo-Erectus just a bipedal primate? He did have an ape-like skull and is said to have still been around some 500 thousand years ago."

"There is no question that the studies of human remains are the most contentious of all the sciences and this is no bad thing. It is an extremely important topic and equally important to get it right. Claims of missing links found, have been made and subsequently dismissed for generations, ever since the search began, and a new human genus has been claimed from just a small scrap of bone, or even a single tooth."

"With regard to the view that bipedalism did not guarantee humans, again, that is only one members opinion and not shared by eminent anthropologists in this country. Our view seems to be that without bipedalism our alleged ancestors could not have become like us."

However, it would seem to be of little use for evolutionary processes to bestow creatures such as the primates with free arms and manipulative fingers, suitable for building and creating, without the bequest of suitable intelligence to make use of them. Both attributes, that is bipedalism and manipulative fingers seemed evident in Homo- Erectus, yet he still had the skull of an ape and an assumed 8 or 900cc of brain material. "We come now to the most amazing and rapid development of human evolutionary processes, that provided in mere thousands of years the great brains of Newton and Einstein, and an increase of a full 500cc of extra brain material, which equates to an amazing 100cc every

100thousand years, yet some 170 million years ago a simple frog had the same body form as it has today, along with fishes fauna flies spiders ants crabs".

"John Willoughby refers to this latter process of human brain development as supernatural evolution and an explanation for it is difficult to find. Along with this major brain development, there was of necessity, other profound genetic change in skull size, and shape shilling with major muscle rerouting and tissue building, all against this backdrop of obvious genetic stability in everything else".

"If as man himself has shown, only controlled genetic change can produce positive results, evident in our animal husbandry techniques and our hybrid creations among flowers and so forth, it must beg the question, what unknown factor controlled the process of human intellectual development?"

"The human is an enigma, a misfit and completely defiant of normal evolutionary processes. If the primary classifications of marine life have kept their same form for a major percentage of the time that earth has been suitably hospitable for the emergence of life, then surely the earth simply isn't old enough for the human brain development to have occurred and achieved natural evolutionary over-endowments."

"We could put this another way. In the 500 million years since the Cambrian explosion of life-forms, the ape amasses 10 billion neurons or brain cells, and the human has 10 times as many, then it would be logical to deduce, he should have needed 10 times as long in order to have attained his 100 billion neurons, one for every star in the galaxy. This would make the human brain appear to be possessing brain material that was evolving five billion years ago. In other words, donated already evolved genetic material provided by some exterior force or unknown variable."

"We cannot even point to a suitable and likely human predecessor that lived before the mysterious appearance of the Cro-Magnon peoples, and certainly none that could possibly have provided the human with such obvious attributes and over-endowments, even to use the term supernatural evolution for human mental development seems like an understatement when we consider the fact that a natural evolution from simian kind would imply that apes were indirectly responsible for the laws of the universe and the theory of relativity. Not only is the human brain over-endowed in its natural state, it is possessed with additional material amounting to some two thirds of its mass, that we must assume one day will be fully utilised. Most certainly ruling out natural selection processes."

"When looking at a typical Neanderthal skull and area of the basic cranium, it is apparent that any verbal skills were almost non-existent. Although the

Neanderthal had a slightly larger brain than modern humans, we must distinguish between size and the infusion of the neurons or cells that contain intelligent genes, otherwise we might expect elephants to rule the world."

Villiers moved to the display screen and produced an image of a Neanderthal skull.

"It can be seen that the Neanderthal skull was longer front to rear, and he was rather beetle-browed and possessed the usual brow ridges and other pithecoid features. But in this typical human skull, (Villiers once again changed the picture) … we see the obvious contrast in the forehead area. Under here," he said, pointing to the forehead, "is the forebrain or new areas of tissue not possessed by the apes. The seat of the higher human functions and the brocas area said to govern the supreme communication abilities of the human."

"This great brain that is housed within this structure is possessed with gifts and abilities that it seems absurd to assume were a bequest from any ape-like ancestor. The ability to envisage and plan future scenarios. Creativity on a scale vastly superior to that required for mere survival. The arts, music, abstract awareness of the beauty of nature, never given a second glance by any other creature. A sense of a higher presence, no matter how we might determine it. To contemplate and peer into the tiniest particles of matter and ponder the far reaches of the universe."

"Watch an ape splitting open a banana and scooping the fruit out, because it has no natural inclination to peel it, after 50 million years of evolution. And try if you will to assume such creatures were responsible indirectly for the brains of Da Vinci Copernicus, Newton, Einstein and other human geniuses."

"Humans have descended to the bottom of the sea, walked on the moon and now contemplate their final frontier. Eventually a means of interstellar travel will be discovered. We have already been endowed with the capacity for mathematics to make it possible. A bequest from whom? If mathematics were necessary for survival on earth, then perhaps apes would be able to count their fingers, after all they've had enough time to be masters of the universe, or at least teaching us in their universities, let alone achieving such a simple task."

"Without mathematics, we would never have been able to envisage a space programme. Orbital insertion and departure and subsequent re-entry require precise mathematical calculations. Are we to conclude from this that the human has been pre-programmed as it were, for space travel? We seem compelled to travel there almost as though it was our destiny."

"We take our intelligence for granted, so much so that certain people see it as simple self-aggrandisement to ponder such things, and obviously do not consider them as a source of wonderment. But the processes of evolution and natural selection have no favourites. Never change for change's sake, never over-endow and are excruciatingly slow and manifest widespread genetic stability. How then can people fail to be surprised or even ponder the reasons why the human so obviously sits apart from it all?"

"Intelligent creative ability in other creatures is all relative to their earthly environment, apes in the trees might pull a few branches over their heads in the rain, but their intellect never develops and improves with age and experience. It would never consider building a dwelling with the materials that surround it. A beaver will build a dam, a bee will construct in clever symmetrical honeycombs. Ants will display intelligence, termites will build an air-conditioned mound, birds build their nests, all activities necessity and essential for their earthly existence."

By no stretch of the imagination could we ever envisage any earthly life form other than humans ever looking up and wondering why the sky is blue, what the stars are, how far away the moon is. The human shows little evidence of being an earthly evolved creature at all. Why haven't all these problems questions and issues been previously debated long before this programme?"

Villiers moved to the table and picked up John's book. "Well, ladies and gentlemen, that is precisely why John Willoughby wrote this book, to promote such discussion and debate that is now actually occurring throughout the media. It was also written with the intention of making it clear to people, that may have been gently conditioned and persuaded over the years, that the question of human origins is largely settled, that this is simply not the case and other alternatives are still open to us for our consideration. And at this point in time, it is unwise to consider that any theory for human origins is written in stone or could be viewed as unassailable."

"The author of this book has worked in primate colonies both here and abroad and makes it clear that there is a world of a difference between what apes will naturally do in their earthly habitat, compared to those who have been cleverly taught special tasks. He sees a process taking place that may possibly be due to our inability to find the conclusive proof that they are our cousins, and as such, is attempting to humanise or force human traits upon them."

"What is the point of teaching chimps to chip stones together to get a sharp flake, so they can cut the string on a box containing fruit, when we would never encounter a chimp in the wild making stone tools. We would not encounter a horse running wild in a pack, suddenly stopping to dance and prance as though it was in an equestrian show or find a seal in a remote colony balancing something on its nose, or a wild elephant stopping to take a bow or stand on one leg."

"Anthropologists often admit, that they do not really know how humans developed their large brains, but as we have pointed out size itself does not seem to be the relevant factor, when the brain of the whale for example weighs in at around 22lbs. What seems to be an important factor, along with the infusion of intelligent genes in the brain cells, is the brain to bodyweight ratio. One might expect a primate alleged relative to be closest to humans in this regard, but it is not the case. The nearest creature is a bird ladies and gentlemen, the common sparrow. Should we then search for a bird like ancestor?" There was a ripple of subdued laughter from the audience. "I don't mean to be flippant ladies and gentlemen." Villiers moved to the table again and picked up a book. "In this work, written by a certain professor Huimar Von Ditfurth, it states that mankind and the chicken had a common ancestor only 280 million years ago. Where did the human get this unexplainable urge to fly? Why is it left to birds such as parrots and mynah birds to imitate human speech when our alleged cousins have neither the intellect or the equipment to try? The human is the only mammal with the larynx low enough in the throat to achieve it. We have already mentioned that the whole picture of evolution in general, is usually presented to us in the form of animated films or diagrams depicting the ancient lungfish slithering out of the primordial seas then going through a whole series of biological transitions or changes from one species to another in order to finally stand upright as humans. Yet the science of biology knows, that creatures cannot change into another species because of the rigid biological chromosome pattern that prevents any chaos resulting from possible inter-species mating. What's more, we cannot produce a particle of evidence to show any sign of transitional stages, or a creature half way between one species and another and in order for the theory to have actually happened, such changes must have occurred. These rigid constraints that determine a species and prevent change are programmed into their DNA molecule and we have to consider why they are so rigid, yet so lax in the past."

"Paleo-anthropologists are all searching for a suitable pro-consul or creature responsible for the emergence of humans on the one hand and modem apes, whatever they might be, on the other. We must surely assume male and female pro-consuls. Do we assume ape-like offspring on the one hand and human-like children on the other? With the ape-like offspring scampering up onto their mother's back and riding around on her while she foraged for food, should have ensured their proliferation and our demise. How did it work so well for the human branch, when, if a human mother left her offspring on the ground after birth, the human race would very quickly cease to exist? How can it be seen as a desirable evolutionary trait, to have not only a complete absence of any protective fur pelt or coat, but for the infant of the human to be completely helpless at birth, when other creatures are up on their feet and feeding totally unaided in a very short time."

"As previously said, the human does not appear to be an earthly evolved creature at all, but instead appears to display features of some super advanced technology, that has by such advancements, made the human offspring totally dependent upon it and long ago removed the primitive basic tendency to fend for oneself, that is evident in every other earthly creature. In short, if humans are an earthly evolved creature, then why do the evolutionary processes fail to look after us when they so obviously do so in every other life form?"

"Humans appeared on earth suddenly and unprepared except for their mental endowments. Such intelligence made them realise other creatures survived the rigours of winter because of their obvious protection. The answer was obvious. As humans had no protection, they had to steal it from other animals or expire, so they promptly set about fashioning weapons and implements to get the job done. There is no earthly reason for apes to make stone tools, they already have their protection. And as for their food, their agile abilities ensure they can climb into the highest branches to get it."

"Those people who look for similarities to humans in chimpanzees should also be prepared to look at the dissimilarities such as the feet, the hands with the different thumb, the barrel chest, long arms, short legs different hips, only suitable for knuckle walking, the pelt, the central nervous system the skull and the jaw, the teeth the tiny brain; in short they are nothing like humans at all."

"We might ask how often had genetic material from our chimpanzee cousins saved human lives in cardiovascular surgery? Why does medical science turn to pigs in this regard? Medical science finds that their physiology is very akin to human and has utilised it for some considerable time."

"And so, ladies and gentlemen, it can be seen, that quite as many questions, anomalies and mysteries require to be addressed in the evolutionary concept for human origins, as we have seen in the belief system of divine human creation. Nevertheless, it is a scientifically logical theory, and no doubt the search will continue for the vital fossil links. Although preoccupied with the African continent in the ever-continuing search, the vital fossils may emerge from somewhere quite different, it could just be a question of time."

Villiers took a sip of water from the tumbler on the dais, then faced the panel again. "Now ladies and gentlemen, it is the turn of the so-called third alternative to be reviewed and it is a belief system with a fairly substantial amount of factors which could be viewed as circumstantial evidence in its favour. It has been in place for decades and has enjoyed the support of a few eminent and academically qualified people. Although when first encountering it, one might view it as sheer science fiction, one quickly realises that the more one reviews all the factors, the more this assumption is dispelled."

"Of course, as a theory for the emergence of humanity, it too can be challenged, criticised and if one wishes, ignored completely. We are free to choose whatever belief system suits us personally. However, one thing that can be said, quite confidently with regard to it, is that it presents itself as a very suitable candidate for the unknown variable or exterior force that Alfred Russell Wallace wrestled with, that may have been responsible for the amazingly over-endowed human brain. It must also be said, that it rather surprisingly allows many of the questions and anomalies regarding our previous two belief systems to fall neatly into place, as though they were factors in an equation, awaiting a common denominator. And the third alternative for human beginnings is that common denominator."

"Briefly, this theory suggests that an extra-terrestrial intelligence encountered earth long in our past and bequeathed the gift of advanced intelligence to humankind by utilizing a suitable donor. Many men of science will immediately write it off as nonsense or consider it as impossible. But we must keep in mind, that the list is quite lengthy of people in the past who felt qualified to state many things were impossible, that have subsequently come to pass. And so, if you would simply remain open minded and consider the theory simply on its merits, as you have done I'm sure, with regard to our two previous belief systems, you will begin to realise this subject is a little more than something straight out of *The X-Files* or a *Star Trek* scenario."

"With our cosmic awareness today, brought about in no small measure by the power of the media and the advances in space technology, taking us on a grand tour of the planets while still in our armchairs, we have a much more enlightened view of what is above us, than for example, a character from biblical times had. However, in order not to lose sight of the objectives in this programme and indeed the book on which it is based, *The Human Enigma*, we should repeat that primarily, this objective, is to simply review all the factors, problems and evidence if any, regarding three distinct belief systems, and hopefully not be seen to encourage or disparage any of them. Your task, as we said at the beginning is simply to assess in terms of sheer logic, and the data presented, which view a super computer might take when evaluating it all. You, ladies and gentlemen are our computer."

"Now, to come to the point, this theory basically, allows for very advanced extra-terrestrial beings not only well versed in all the known sciences, but with a knowledge of medical science and genetic blending, enormously more advanced than our own, and biological knowledge of every earthly strain, and possibly other worlds containing life forms also. And all these assumptions are of course perfectly feasible. Knowledge may be finite there could be other world entities who have learned everything there is to know. After all the list of elements is probably finite. Eventually every atomic and subatomic particle would be known, we may eventually have the ability to rearrange matter by changing its atomic number. Recently a gene has been isolated that is said to govern intelligence. A successful head transplant has been carried out on a monkey. We will grow human organs such as the heart in laboratories. The isolation of all known genes for every trait and malady will come under human control and manipulation."

"The worst-case scenario of the church, with regard to satanic science as it used to be viewed, will have come to pass. Man will challenge the creator by becoming creators of life themselves. Yet for all that, humans are hardly out of the stone age in certain earthly zones, while other areas plan trips to Mars. But the same situation existed of course when the ancient Egyptians were planning their pyramids in comparison to the ancient people of many other lands on earth at that time."

"Consider the reign of the dinosaurs, which lasted some 180 million years! No intelligent creative beings on earth at all. If we only assign a couple of million years to our own evolution, how many other-world intelligences could have evolved in that enormous period of time? We are striving to find the means of interstellar rather than interplanetary power, and no doubt we will eventually succeed. Other intelligent life could have done so long ago."

"As previously stated, there are more stars than there are grains of sand on every beach on earth, of course, they are not all sun-like stars. Some are so huge, that if our world was orbiting at the same distance as it does from our own sun, the entire sky would be filled with its image. Even a favourable star like our own has only one planet out of nine with life on it. Nevertheless, it would seem to be quite preposterous to assume ours is the only populated world in the universe."

"And so, by sheer logic, we can set the stage for such a thing as extra-terrestrial biogenetic creation to have been possible. After all, we only have to reflect on where our own advancements are taking us. Long into the future, humans may kindly bequeath the gift of intelligence to lesser mortals on some far-off world. Nevertheless, for all our logical assumptions, there are still people on earth who feel they are suitably qualified to write it off as impossible. They will be judged by history just as others are today. For example, the academic who firmly and confidently stated 'there are no stones in the sky therefore stones cannot fall from the sky."

"If by some amazingly advanced genetic process, intelligent genes were suffused into the creature selected on earth by our hypothetical ET's then it is perfectly possible that memory genes were also infused and as such, may be responsible for humans re-inventing things on earth achieved by the donors long ago. Human geniuses have emerged out of their time so to speak, such as Leonardo Da Vinci or the ancient alchemists who were the physicists of their time. If they had possessed the ability to subtract one proton and three neutrons from mercury, they could have succeeded in their quest to make their gold. Have humans misunderstood the command to go forth and multiply and only considered it to be in an earthly environment? Whichever way we interpret the Garden of Eden, it was a purposely selected earthly zone where men were made just as every other earthly legend tells of gods or sky people making men."

"Why would humans be suitably equipped, pre-programmed and mentally qualified to envisage and bring about space travel if it were not meant to be? It is comparatively easy for our technologically advanced times to theorise on ET. biogenetic creation. After all, we have acted like such beings ourselves towards cattle and plants on a smaller scale, producing hybrids and so forth. How profound to consider that we ourselves could be hybrids? "What prompted the late Charles Fort who lived earlier in the century, to suggest humankind could be property."

"The angels of the bible who we could assume were the descendants of the original creators of 'let us make men in our image' fame, certainly treated early human creations rather like property, only fit to be destroyed in large numbers, due to faulty behaviour patterns. In terms of cold logic, this might have been the only way that prevented them from passing on their genetic faults, and the few that were saved such as Noah were superhuman and this was evident in their lifespan. They lived for centuries. If this was some crude genetic cleansing exercise, how would human behaviour with regard to manifestations of negative and more undesirable traits be assessed today by the hypothetical descendants of the original creators, who could be manifesting their presence in the mysterious UFO phenomena? We have to consider if any other plans are being formulated for us."

"A certain Dr. M. Jacobs who has made an intensive study of the abduction phenomenon is convinced that some of his subjects experienced actual alien abduction and genetic analysis. Abductions are not only alleged in recent times, the phenomenon is almost as old as written history, even occurring in the bible with Elijah's trip up into the sky in a whirlwind. If one did give any credence to the theory of alien genetic creation, then it would be a natural assumption that humans would be required to be analysed from time to time, over lengthy periods, in order to analyse their genetic mental development. Dr. Jacobs finds from his studies, that another major hybrid creation plan could be in process. Are the creators trying to breed out all the negative genes that seem to be holding back human mental maturity? For all our fantastic technological advancements and positive achievements, we still happily slaughter our fellow men in stupid futile wars and conflagrations."

"Obviously, science is quite comfortable with the idea of extra-terrestrial intelligence existing on other worlds, otherwise large sums would not be sanctioned to finance S.E.T.I programmes to search for them. It has even been suggested that the S.E.T.I. programme is part of an intensive ruse or cover up on the lines of, 'if we are still searching for them, we can't have alien life forms floating in preserving fluid from crash retrievals such as the Roswell incident, can we?' Nothing will sway the ufologists that an intense cover up has not or indeed is not taking place."

"One cannot but sympathise with them and their views. How so? You may ask. Well…after the freedom of information act in the USA was passed, thousands of documents suddenly appeared that the various authorities had previously stated they didn't have. What's more, black felt tip deletions made these documents almost unreadable but obviously quite readable on the retained copies, which of course, *makes* it quite evident that not only was there a cover up but there still obviously is."

"Having established then, by sheer logic that there is a cover up, what is the extent of it? How much do they really know? The Roswell incident will probably never be solved as fewer and fewer people exist who had any first-hand knowledge of it, and certain data can be highly classified for up to one hundred years, perhaps indefinitely."

"However, in order to keep to our objective in dealing with this belief system for human origins, the Roswell incident is not only interesting but quite relevant. A fairly recent film, shown on a major television network, clearly suggested that the death of the US Defence Secretary of the time of the alleged Roswell crash retrieval, of a UFO and its occupants in 1947, that is, James Forrestal, may not have been suicide at all but something far more sinister. The film made it clear that he was one of the groups that the ufologists call the Majestik Twelve and that he had actually visited the zone where a still living alien was kept. The message came across very clearly in the film that alien intelligence had in fact altered human evolution. Contrary to the views of the rest of the group. James Forrestal felt that this profound information should become public knowledge."

"Of course, this was not the only film that has inferred this alien genetic creation idea. Another movie called Hangar 18 did precisely the same thing. It can be seen therefore that it is not a new idea, and nearly three decades ago, a NASA scientist and a Doctor of Mathematics stated the following. - Villiers moved to the dais and sifted through some papers and picked up a written quotation."

"This book is concerned with the strong possibility, almost a probability in our measured opinions, that mankind on earth may have had super intelligent ancestors from outer space and that man may be a hybrid, partly of terrestrial origin and partly extraterrestrial. End of quote." "The mathematician who was the co-author went on to say, "if extra-terrestrials have visited earth they would be possessed with the capacity for mathematics, that is why I consider the human capacity for mathematics to be an indication that humans are not only of earthly origin.' "Quite an astounding assumption from this learned man."

"Ours is a comparatively young and quite unspectacular star system. Some stars and assumed planetary systems have lived their lives and expired before our solar system even formed. The dinosaurs expired 65 million years ago and were said to have existed for 160 million years. This makes the period of their initial emergence over 220 million years ago. Conditions were just as suitable then for humans to have emerged at that point instead of our assumed beginnings. What if we had emerged then and managed to survive the dinosaurs? What would we now be capable of ?"

"How would we be able to deal with creatures that were so far advanced? Did they come to earth long ago and make men in their image just as every earthly legend suggests? To be sure we haven't heard a peep out of anyone else during the thirty years or so of the SETI programmes, unless of course they have decided not to tell us. However, bleeping out a signal on a common and expected frequency such as the hydrogen spectral line, may have been a feature of ET's development long before we even existed, and their radiations may have swept over our world long ago when no-one was here to listen. But just arriving in earth space would have been a major achievement for them, let alone jiggling about with our DNA and creating men in their image."

"Nevertheless, we have to concede that such creatures could exist. It is suggested that they would not look anything like us, but why not? The evolutionary process on earth seems to be struggling to produce the seemingly ideal body form for creative manipulation and fingers with manual dexterity. Rearing up on two legs, the minimum requirement for locomotion Freeing the arms and hands to bring food to the mouth rather than the vulnerability of lowering the head to eat. Eyes moving to the front to observe and assist the hands in their creative manipulations. The universe is predominantly made up of hydrogen, but the heavy elements are probably similar on other worlds, and the many sun-like stars we can observe could well have earth like worlds if favourably positioned in the habitability zone of their star."

"The weather systems, lightning, seas and photosynthesising, production of amino acids necessary to get life going, may all have occurred along similar lines to our own. We don't know how universal the life processes may be, because we cannot go and look for ourselves, but creatures who have possessed the ability to go and look, for millennia, may have brought their own influences to bear on other worlds and just as our own legends suggest, brought other life forms and crops to earth in the process."

"The scientists and astrophysicists envisage terra-forming other worlds such as Mars or Venus for human occupation, by introducing micro-organisms such as blue/green algae to get the life process started. This substance is found in abundance in earth's most ancient rocks which of course begs the question could earth have been terraformed for subsequent life forms three and a half billion years ago? If creative intelligence existed then, what would they now have become?

"They ought to have discovered every particle, every element, know everything there is to know and may have dispensed with body forms long ago and may be pure creative energy or spirit and travel the length and breadth of the universe. It doesn't seem likely that we could know how to deal with such an intelligence, but they may quite easily know how to deal with us."

"However, beings that may only be a mere thousand years ahead of us would still be enormously more advanced than ourselves. Particularly if their scientific advancements have proceeded at a pace similar to our own. Only one planet out of nine in our own system favourable for the emergence of life, cuts down the odds-on life elsewhere to some degree, but they ought to exist by sheer weight of numbers. Clearly, the first priority on the visiting aliens' list would be an intense analysis of earthly microbes and whether theirs could affect us. They would not wish for every life form on earth to expire before they even got a chance to analyse them."

"H.G. Wells' Martians, for all their efforts in getting to earth, singularly failed to do this and afford any protection for themselves from our common cold germs. If the various flu germs can lay people on earth low so effectively; those who are born here, with a fairly good resistance built in, then it would seem that they would be absolutely deadly to alien creatures unfamiliar with them."

"It would seem logical to suppose, that any visiting ET's with the knowledge and advancements necessary to alter human evolution, would have also visited other worlds and may be familiar with all the biological life forms if any, and all the microbes on those worlds on the camel route to earth. They may see it as their clear duty to promote and create intelligence in any suitable creatures best equipped by their planetary evolution to utilise it. And when we ourselves have isolated every gene and attained full control and manipulation of them, we may also dispense with any retarding and troublesome ethics and create on a grand scale by manipulating the genes of the primates to utilise them as intelligent helpers.

In other words, we ourselves are rushing headlong into a situation where we would be doing exactly what is hypothesised for our own presence here on earth."

"Is it possible that the first experiment began with Homo-Erectus? The Neanderthals followed them and did indeed have suddenly larger brains, but the rest of their body form left much to be desired. Were they viewed as an experimental failure and manipulated to extinction by the infusion of retrogressive genes? The fossil finds would tend to support this assumption to some degree. The later finds seem less evolutionarily advanced than earlier ones. The Neanderthals were a failure by any of our accepted views of human emergence."

"Another theory mentioned in John Willoughby's book for our beginnings, indeed the entire range of earthly life forms, is the view held by some scientists that the entire process may have begun simply by a coincidental biological accident and may never be repeated elsewhere in the universe. Of course, natural evolution would be simply a result of this, so it isn't really a separate theory, but it is a valid viewpoint. However, the life force seems so insistent and prolific, that with the right planetary conditions, the major consensus would view it as more of an inevitability than an accident."

"But if the life force is so insistent, where is everybody? We haven't heard a peep out of anyone (at least that we have been told about) in the 50 plus years since the SETI programme began."

"The discoveries in astrophysics make it a very uncertain science, and viewpoints and theories are continually being reviewed, changed or having to be disposed of altogether. One strange feature of it all is that primarily, most discoveries teach us really how much we don't know. The universe is said to be not only stranger than we imagine, but stranger than we can imagine. Even our own moon a mere quarter of a million miles away, has produced, after six manned missions there, and hundreds of pounds of its material now in our laboratories, more questions than there are answers."

"The nearest star to us is Proxima Centauri and that star orbits another pair or binary system. So, the whole system is a triple arrangement. We could get there in a mere 40 years travelling at only a quarter of the speed of light, if we had the suitable power sources. But what would we find if we did go there? What kind of gravitational disturbance would attendant planets experience there? Could life evolve with all that tugging and heaving going on? Perhaps so. Perhaps it would have even better and more prolific growth of vegetation and fauna, with all that permanent sunlight and subsequent photosynthesis going on, if a moist suitably positioned world does exist there." "But if we are the first, then at the current rate of technological advancement, it seems almost inevitable humans will go forth and multiply on worlds perhaps very far from earth long into the future."

"However, to return to the point of our possible hybrid ancestry, due to genetic manipulation. It does seem strange that even earthly legend from such widely separated areas should all be stating that God, gods or sky people made us. One of the oldest legends from Sumeria states quite specifically that men were made to bear the burden of creation; in other words, we were created by a process, where the ultimate aim was for humans to become creators of life themselves, and this will surely come to pass."

"If SETI is simply an expensive ruse as has been suggested, to promote the idea that as we are still looking, we can't have any little green men from UFO crash retrievals floating in preserving fluid, then it would be amazing to assume that governments would go to such lengths to keep such information from us. What if we did have to dump all our history and preconceived notions, which would be particularly relevant if such creatures did alter human evolution? Surely that is better than to continue to amass false data and beliefs. Surely by now modem humanity is mentally ready for such possible revelations, surely, we could handle it? People of 150 years ago, comfortable with the assumption that the hand of God created them, must have suffered and survived the cultural shock and social disorientation when told their ancestors were apes and not Adam and Eve."

"If there are no aliens in earth space and never have been, and SETI is genuine, how wise are we being to announce our presence in such cavalier fashion?" "We cannot guarantee aliens will all be peaceful and benign. Humans stand on the brink of deep space travel and even interstellar travel in the not too distant future. Yet we still slaughter each other here on earth."

"It would seem that aggressive genes, unless purposely bred out of us, will always ensure humans behave in such a manner. Commercial exploitation and gain ensured radio was developed as quickly as possible and no serious thoughts went into the fact that radiations of an intelligent nature would be leaving earth at the speed of light. Our radiations are now sweeping over other worlds and possible alien receivers some 90 light years away from earth, in a great expanding bubble."

"It isn't science fiction to surmise that plans could be in the process or being laid this very moment to come and investigate the source. How do we know that their intentions are strictly honourable? For all our science and advancements humans have hardly stepped forward one metre in eliminating the aggressive tendencies of a tribal group of ancestors who decided to pick up animal bones and beat their adversaries with them. Before we achieve the ability to leave for the stars, we will have terraformed Venus and Mars and plundered their resources, and maybe even polluted and despoiled them, as well as earth."

"We may have to find another home. There may be civilisations in this condition who may suddenly start receiving intelligent signals from earth. Who have also achieved the power sources to come and size up earth as ripe for the taking. All they would need to do, would be to direct a couple of choice asteroids our way and wait for the birds who would probably be the only creatures to survive, to clean everything up for them."

"To return to the subject of the third alternative or alien biogenetic creation, for how we came to be, some people have considered this theory, and felt suitably qualified to deem it impossible. In the first place, history is littered with scholars and academics who have made such dogmatic statements regarding things that subsequently came to pass. The only thing impossible regarding this theory, is that it is impossible to state categorically that it didn't happen."

"ET's clever enough to get here, then pull off such an achievement would also be clever enough to successfully keep it from us until they felt we were ready to receive such profound revelations. People who state that a thing is impossible should at least be gracious enough to add, impossible for us here on earth at our current rate of advancement."

"What then is the circumstantial evidence in support of this theory? And just how strong is it? If such hypothetical ET's did alter our evolution by advanced genetic means, then this amazing, purposeful and quite profound act would immediately tie them to earth or at least the descendants of the original creators for thousands of years of human development. They would be responsible for us and our behaviour patterns. They would be observed coursing through our skies in an ongoing UFO phenomenon for as long as our written history existed."

"There would be human abductions for analysis of our development in an ongoing process also appearing in our written history since it emerged. There would still be a continuing abduction programme today. Ladies and gentlemen, evidence for all of the aforesaid does exist. Certain learned gentlemen, among them doctors and professors, have carried out an extensive study of the alleged alien abductions and at least one of them is convinced that it is happening. Even that hybrids, which of course we ourselves would be, due to their initial actions, are being and have been created for decades."

"With their aforesaid responsibility for humanity, if such a profound creation programme had occurred in some alien Garden of Eden on earth, they would see it as a clear duty, to eliminate our aggressive and savage tendencies by further advanced means. And these new hybrids may well be part of that plan."

"Those who accept religious biblical teachings are happy to accept that their chosen creator carried out such means of achieving the same end by the mass Elimination of faulty creations, saving only a few who would beget more of their kind for a future world. If alien creatures do exist in our earth space, then we must hope that they do not consider adopting such crude methods to rectify the mistakes of their forebears. Interestingly, regarding the subject of human abductions, they go back not only to biblical times with one or two events which could be interpreted as such, but even earlier, in certain Sumerian writings such as the Epic of Gilgamesh."

"Any ET intelligence encountering earth and new life forms to analyse would also abduct, but not in an ongoing programme. They would only need a few examples of the primary classifications of races on earth, to learn all they needed to know about human physiology. We have to consider the possibility that the angels of biblical times could well have been hybrid creations themselves and utilised to achieve the ends of the creators by being acceptable enough in their appearance to interact with humans." "It has even been seriously suggested by those people studying the abduction phenomenon, that this is precisely what is happening today. The so-called ufologists leave also suggested that the strange beings known as M.I.B's or men in black are such an example of hybrid humanoid types and in their case, simply utilised to gather information on what exactly the human observers who had reported a UFO close encounter, had actually seen."

"The first two prerequisites that we would have to take on board before even considering this amazing proposition, would be the possibility of another world intelligence existing, and that at least one would be further advanced than ourselves. Two very easy factors to accept. With all the fantastic things to come in our own scientific advancements, it is easy to conjecture that they could have been achieved elsewhere in the cosmos long ago.

'We know that intelligent life does exist in space...us...we ourselves are proof of this simple fact. How many alien eyes could be right now looking at a twinkling star in their night sky that could be our sun? Of course, many people seriously believe that they are here already and have been for some considerable time."

"To return to the analysis and study of the abduction phenomenon and its implications. The victims or abductees are not for the most part crackpots or eccentrics. Many are intelligent people holding good positions, who did not initially want to talk about it and wish it had never happened to them.

Psychiatrists, some with the ability of hypnotic regression and applying it to the victims in order to make them re-experience their encounters. Usually after taking all the trouble to regress them, refuse still to believe it actually happened to their subjects, but that the subjects merely firmly believe that it did, and it is only the belief that emerges which makes one wonder why they bother to do it in the first place."

"Our earlier considerations, concerning alien microbes and their possible effects, and of course ours, regarding their physiology, must again come into the picture. As far as is known, no victim of an alleged abduction has contracted an incurable alien disease, and where they could study and protect themselves from our bacteria, they couldn't immunise the whole world from theirs. This problem would be more prevalent with abductors that had encountered earth, but had no hand in human development, but on the other hand, hypothetical descendants of the possible creators would know that our biological immune systems would be a product of the bio- engineering skills of their life forms or more specifically, their forebears."

"Therefore, we may already have the same immunity or resistance to alien bacteria as they have, which of course, if the abductions are really happening, would indicate the abductors are genetically linked to humans. All of his of course sounds very science fiction-like, not to say imaginative and farfetched, but in dealing with this topic, these incursions are necessary to be made in an open-minded way, if we are to analyse it at all."

"If humanity is the result of an alien genetic experiment and it could be suggested that the fossil evidence supports it, we would have to concede that a very long presence in earth space would have been necessary by the alleged creators or gods, who made men in their image. of course, even this assumption could be challenged with the introduction of the so-called Einsteinian time dilation theory, which holds that if a space craft departed earth at a speed approaching that of light, time would slow down enormously for the occupants of the craft but pass by normally on earth."

"If Neanderthal was viewed as a failure, and purposely genetically retrogressed to ensure his demise, this is certainly reflected in the fossil finds where the later bone fossils appear more pithecoid than the earlier ones. By correct manipulation of the chromosome pattern, these hypothetical creators could also ensure no chaotic mixing was introduced into their experimental programme by ensuring Neanderthal and their next possible creation Cro-Magnon, could not interbreed and the evidence is that they did not and could not. And as already made clear to you, compelling Human fossil links are almost non-existent. Instead, all we have, as one famous anthropologist put it, is 'a meagre fragmented array of isolated teeth and bones and portions of skulls.' And of course, in spite of our assumptions regarding the creatures themselves, they could simply have belonged to another variety of primate now extinct, rather than an indisputable human ancestor.

"If one was to give credence to this ET biogenetic creation theory and its apparent supportive circumstantial evidence or factors, then one such factor would be the bone fossil evidence being so scrappy and incomplete. And more evident of some kind of experimentation, than one predecessor developing gradually refined attributes, and its successor even more so. In other words, reflecting the Darwinian ideal. Another would be the strange similarity of every earthly legend referring to a creation scenario by 'God, or some lesser gods."

"Further supporting factors would be the longevity of the UFO phenomenon and especially the ongoing abductions, indicating a form of progress check or analysis of human development. Other supporting factors would be the studies of the DNA of human blood and mitochondrial DNA, refuting ancient simian ancestry, plus there are the strange events in the bible referring to genetic creation of special beings including Jesus himself, the angels, and their aerial activity. All these factors could be put in as parts of a larger equation, with the common denominator of course being ET biogenetic creation of humanity."

"Strangely, no concerted effort was ever made in order to study these contributory factors. Even the most common factor, which of course is the UFO phenomenon, is still dealt with in a rather tongue in cheek way by the media, and the view is, that it is all a natural phenomenon that our physics cannot yet explain. Of course, this would hold up if all the reports were merely regarding dancing lights and so forth but some involve people's encounters with obvious controlled structured craft and sometimes their occupants."

"Nobody will fund serious scientific research into it, yet funds are readily available for a search for ET. Do these people who sanction the funds expect ET's only to reside hundreds of light years away and all be less advanced than ourselves and couldn't possibly be able to cross interstellar space simply because we can't? If science is happy enough to look for evidence of ET's what is the problem with looking for them closer to home, when such an abundance of evidence seems to be staring them straight in the face?"

"When we dealt with the aforementioned Condon report, Professor Condon was selected for his well-known cynical and sceptical attitude toward it all. The end result was the rather contradictory conclusion that further study of it would not further the cause of science, and that it is a phenomenon not yet understood by our current knowledge of physics and as said, what this basically states therefore, is that we don 't understand it, but further study would not help us to understand it"

"Unfortunately for the US air force and indeed for every other air force, the phenomenon did not go away. In fact, statistics show, that it increased with regard to the volume of reports." "It has been said, that any thoughts of super advanced extra-terrestrial creators are simply a search for a God substitute. Yet the theory of Charles Darwin was itself accepted as a God substitute by science, as it offered a more logical and scientific explanation for the appearance of humankind than biblical creation."

"However, the theory of evolution and natural selection also helped to explain the other ancient fossil forms, and obvious great age of the earth that had previously been calculated by a certain Bishop Usher to be only a mere 4000 or so years old."

"Clearly logical conclusion rather than fantasy is always preferable when considering these matters related to the earth, and the creatures that walk upon it such as we, but logic may seem correct and acceptable in one particular era, but silly with the benefit of hindsight in a later, more technologically advanced era. A good example is the aforesaid statement 'there are no stones in the sky, therefore stones cannot fall from the sky.' Who, at the time was brave enough to dispute it?"

"The fact is, this so-called third alternative for human origins could be solved and proven at a stroke, if the allegations made in the aforementioned film dealing with the allegedly true crash retrieval event, at Roswell New Mexico in 1947 were proven to be true and more importantly, released to the public." "But who would wish to be the government saddled with the responsibility to release such information?"

"It would seem then, that the UFO phenomenon and our correct interpretation of it, is one of the key factors in this problem. It would be astounding enough if ET's were in earth space let alone having in effect produced humanity. Yet it is surprising how people in general, react to it in such a variety of ways."

"For example, a sighting was reported near the house of a well-known politician. When asked to comment, he said 'I have much more important things to concern myself with than UFO's." "We think we know what he meant, but it we analyse his comment and consider how profound a revelation it would be if UFO's are controlled structured craft from an 'otherworld' technology, it would appear that a forthcoming general election was higher on the politician's agenda."

"One might suppose, that the reason most people can deal so easily with the possibility of ET's moving about above us, or appear slightly bemused by it, is because most of us don't really believe it. But if it was revealed to be true, some of us may not be able to mentally handle it at all. The various authorities would of course be well aware of this, and with their proclivity in any case toward secrecy, there would quite easily be the tendency towards a cover up, especially in regard to such a profound revelation concerning our own origins, and our established beliefs." "If we would have so much trouble with the UFO phenomenon itself becoming fact, how could we hope to handle revelations of ET biogenetic creation of our forebears?"

"Of course, the new Messiah, Charles Darwin, shocked many people 160 years ago with his theorising and got away with it and received many lukewarm Christians, struggling to accept mind-stretching biblical teachings to his banner, and of course all those with atheistic viewpoints to begin with. But has he led them into a wilderness of doubt and uncertainty? After all, he had his own escape clause by stating 'if the fossil links are not found then the theory falls down,' but subjects had in some cases abandoned their former beliefs, and at that time had nowhere else to turn if the theory remained unproven."

"Today however, if they so wish, they could embrace this third alternative for their origins, which has at least some evidence, albeit circumstantial that appears to support it." "How much support then, over the years, has this third alternative actually had among scholars and academics? Well… it is fairly well known that the late Professor Carl Sagan once said that an extra-terrestrial intelligence could have visited earth in our past. However, he seemed to spend the rest of his life regretting that he said it, and often appeared on tire side of the debunkers on prime-time TV slots when the UFO phenomenon was dealt with."

"During the late 60's and throughout the 70's the ancient astronaut theme was well in vogue, and paperbacks were rolling off the presses dealing with the topic. But the book by the NASA scientist and the mathematician quoted to you earlier, was different in respect to the ET creation theory. Probably for the first time, the shortcomings of the entire Darwinian theory were highlighted, and it was made clear that with a little imagination and open mindedness, their own theory was just as feasible as any other for human origins."

"The UFO phenomenon is certainly resolved and will not go away. Some scientists take the view that if ET's are not present then they jolly well ought to be. The great age of the universe and the comparatively young age of our own solar system allows for many advanced technological societies to have arisen around older stars."

The famous Drake equation formulated by the team of scientists who formed the original SETI team, led by Professor Frank Drake figured that there ought to be around a million intelligent civilisations in our galaxy alone, and of course there are many billions of galaxies."

"In considering the longevity once again of the UFO phenomenon and the alleged abductions, both could be interlinked and key factors in our third alternative. However, it would seem, that no matter how convincing the alleged abductions are, most of those who deal with the phenomena, with a couple of exceptions, mostly take the view that the abductions are entirely from the abductees' own heads. If so, this would be a little worrying in terms of the mental condition of a good portion of the human race, many of whom hold down good responsible jobs."

"To consider another factor in the equation that might add up to our third alternative, we must again consider the similarity of every earthly legend asserting men were made by god- or sky people. it -could be stretching coincidence enormously for this to have been a chance happening. If an otherworld intelligence did produce the Aurignacion peoples who seem to arrive from nowhere, upright, intelligent, creative with artistic gifts and so forth, and perhaps most importantly to the theory, had no predecessor, the first lessons they would be given would be in communicative speech."

"The first true humans had the larynx low in the throat unlike other mammals, also they had been equipped with the forebrain, which is new tissue and governs our higher functions. Speech is said to be controlled from an area of this portion of the brain totally absent in our alleged predecessors and known as the Broca's area. There would-be no-good reason for the theoretical biogenetic creators to hide the facts of the first anatomically modem human's creation from them. Indeed, they may have had it specifically explained to them."

"If it took place at all, then it must have been in a specific earthly zone which we could call Eden. Before any thoughts or considerations regarding writing and recording history, every scrap of knowledge would be handed down from generation to generation by word of mouth, and as such would become distorted and embellished over the millennia but would retain the basic core factor of creation by God or gods, and this is the situation we are in today."

"It is interesting to contemplate, that no earthly legend states that creatures were created that ultimately turned into men. If one subscribes to this theory. then clearly the event can be determined once we agree on the date of appearance of the anatomically modern Cro-Magnon Aurignacion peoples.

However, this would not be acceptable for obvious reasons in considering the time period for divine human creation which is alleged in Christian doctrines to have occurred when everything else was created."

"Nevertheless, we have to consider that Adam and Eve were anatomically modern arid attractive humans and not grotesque hominids or ugly Neanderthals causing the circumstantial evidence to lean more toward the third alternative. rather than divine creation."

"Another factor to consider when looking at this rather fantastic hypothesis is that although we can rightly point to the major over-endowment of the human brain at its best, we must also consider the negative and retarding qualities of the human at its worst, and in this regard, neither a divine creator or a hypothetical ET creator could be expected to be entirely satisfied with their handiwork. And as we previously assessed, with regard to belief in a divine creator, religious teachings are already in place that allow for the traumatic second coming with a host of angels to separate the righteous from the wicked"

"Does this mean that in the latter assumption, a host of ET's will arrive to genetically modify all human firstborn and by advanced genetic means eliminate all our negative and aggressive genes? A natural responsibility for negative human behaviour, would lie squarely with the descendants of the original creators, that is the little green men; or more specifically grey men, alleged to be in our airspace today and still hauling great numbers of humans up into their craft for analysis."

"We could take some comfort from the thought, that even if this amazing hypothesis was true, there may not be a requirement at all for further genetic manipulation within the brain. After all, along with its normal over-endowment it seems to have additional and currently still undeveloped areas, that one could assume will one day become fully utilised. Perhaps the brain will self-regulate itself, and development of these areas will be when the human reaches a higher mental state of maturity and becomes fully civilised and the constant abductions are simply routine analysis to ensure these dormant areas of the human brain are developing."

David Villiers moved to the table and took a sip of water, then turned to the panel again. "Well ladies and gentlemen, there it is the third alternative for human origins. As amazing as it is we cannot simply dismiss it or assume the rather arrogant stance that only humans and our science, could ever reach the stage of advancement to do such things. We may, at the current rate of advancement in genetic science, quite soon become creators of life itself and assume one day, suitable means to traverse interstellar space will be discovered all the conditions will be in place for humans to be doing exactly what the theory suggests for our own appearance on earth."

"So then, as we approach the end of the presentation of the data, and before we ask you to consider the most logical belief system of the three presented to you. We will conclude by displaying a list of items which appear to be the major factors or circumstantial evidence in support of this so-called, third alternative. Villiers moved to the display screen and began pressing various buttons on a panel below it. He was preparing the list of data for his concluding part of the programme."

All in the household of John Willoughby had been totally captivated by Villiers' presentation. It had all flowed smoothly without any problems. Not like in the studio where John had observed all the cuts, out-takes and interruptions of one form or another. He stretched his legs and glanced at his family. He felt sure they all wished to leave the room, and even though it was being recorded they had all remained seemingly riveted to the screen.

David Villiers had picked up the press switch on the end of a thin cable and held it in his left hand. Half turned to the display screen, they began to speak after the screen lit up. "Ladies and gentlemen, before you retire and attempt your difficult task of trying to beach a logical decision according to the evidence presented to you tonight. I would like, as a finale to this section of the programme, to go through this list of factors, that as a whole could be viewed as supporting evidence albeit circumstantial, for another, or third alternative for how we humans came to be."

As the data began to roll up the screen rather like credits, Villiers read it out to the audience;

"One- 160 years ago Charles Darwin introduced an alternative to divine creation doctrines, by stating chimpanzees and gorillas were man's closest living relatives and we are the product of evolution and natural selection from primate ancestors."

"Two- Theory embraced by science but could not be tested as not a single ancient fossil had been found at the time."

"Three- Charles Darwin's contemporary Alfred Russell Wallace diverts from the theory. Seeks some unknown variable as being responsible for the human mental development and over-endowed brain, developed in advance of its needs for the mere survival of a naked ape, as nature never over-endows."

"Four- Human brain has great capacity for mathematics, unnecessary for survival yet very necessary for space travel."

"Five- Human compulsion to travel into the cosmos."

"Six - 150 years after Darwinian theory introduced, vital fossil links still not found."

"Seven - Darwin's statement under review 'if the fossil links are not found, the theory falls down."

"Eight - Human fossil record appears more akin to an experiment than the ever scrutinizing and improving process favoured by Darwin."

"Nine - No viable family tree can be constructed going back to the strange pithecoid predecessors of anatomically modern humans."

"Ten - Complete assemblies constructed of 65-million-year-old animal bones in our museums but not a single 100% complete skeleton of an indisputable ancestor."

"Eleven - Up to 100 thousand years ago anatomically modern humans appear, already evolved with no predecessor, upright, artistic and creatively intelligent."

"Twelve - Science fails to support theory. DNA of human blood shows no connection with previous apes and bipeds and studies of mitochondrial DNA show recent origin for mankind."

"Thirteen - Obvious genetic stability for many millions of years in everything else except the human."

"Fourteen - Human brain develops an extra 500cc's of brain material from demise of Homo-erectus who possessed some 900cc's only 500 thousand years ago but still pithecoid. Major genetic change in skull shape muscle rerouting and additional tissue building in human forebrain. Additional brain material provided but still unutilised, totally defying natural selection processes."

"Fifteen - Profound human qualities impossible to envisage as a simian bequest."

"Sixteen - After 50 million years of evolution from earliest primates, apes fail to develop other than primitive prerequisites for their survival."

"Seventeen - Every earthly legend from widely separated areas contains racial memory of men made or created by God or lesser gods."

"Eighteen - Entities accepted as angels descend and ascend on pillars of fire in biblical texts. Clearly defined accounts of creation and genetic husbandry evident in Old Testament. Moving stars and obvious aerial activity evident."

"Nineteen - Mysterious aerial objects evident in writings since history first recorded."

"Twenty - Alleged and ongoing abductions into aerial craft. Strange creatures evidently examining human development."

Villiers presses the button on the end of the cable and the screen goes blank.

"Well there it is ladies and gentlemen, it is for you to decide what you think it all adds up to. You may find it easy to find alternative explanations for all this, or you may consider that it cannot all be simply dismissed as coincidence or meaningless. You may ask has such an evaluation of all these factors already taken place behind closed doors as it were.   The ufologists always maintain that governments covering up the facts. If the authorities have computed the result that conforms with this so-called third alternative for human origins, then this would, as said, most certainly be a compelling reason for any alleged cover up than that UFO's may be controlled structured craft."

"Well ladies and gentlemen, that concludes my presentation of the three primary belief systems mostly subscribed to in the western world, for how we humans came to be. I ask you now to retire and consider your verdict or on which theory appears, in your opinion, to shine out above the others as the most compelling according to the evidence. Over to you, our panel."

The programme faded out and a caption appeared that stated "Part Two of our programme and the verdict of the panel, all follow after the news.'

John Willoughby's family began to stretch and stir. Carol was the first to speak. "I'll get some coffee." As she arose and headed for the kitchen she paused, and looked back at John and said, "I have a confession to make." John looked surprised and said, "What's that darling?" Carol replied, "I haven't actually read my copy of your book." "Whaaaat!" John exclaimed, staring wide eyed and feigning anger. She grinned and said, "Well, I thought it might be heavy going. But I think now, after David's presentation, I'll understand it better." Carol disappeared into the kitchen and the boys also left the room.

John looked at the face down copy of his book *The Human Enigma* on the small table to right. He picked it up and read the publishers' blurb on the rear cover; "150 years after Darwin set down his theory of human evolution the vital fossils still elude us… so begins *The Human Enigma*, a truly epic enquiry into the origins of our race. In particular it examines the human brain, seen as a uniquely wonderful creation, which seems to be a gift from God. Or was it a gift from the gods? Besides Darwinian evolution, this book examines another theory to explain the questions surrounding our origins. The fantastic proposition that mankind may have been a biogenetic creation by ET intelligences who have appeared in human history as gods, creators, and now mysterious observers, that appear to be continually abducting human specimens worldwide in an ongoing programme of analysis regarding human genetic development. The strange paradox emerges in this work, that the most fantastic theory for human origins, appears to have the most compelling evidence, albeit of the circumstantial kind, in its favour."

John put the book down and tried to put himself in the position of the average member of the panel. What could they deduce from all that Villiers had presented to them? Although they were chosen in a street survey for their apparent neutrality on the issue and articulate intelligent replies to certain questions, they probably all had some kind of belief or notion regarding their beginnings. John was well aware that his own profession had quietly conditioned many people that a natural evolution from the primates was all but certain by assumptive statements and conjecture, and their rare statements of perplexity were only written in certain works that the layman, unless he takes the time to study them, does not encounter.

The retiring panel as part of their brief had been encouraged to suppress any preconceived notions or beliefs lurking beneath their chosen neutrality. But people cannot switch: off like machines. Ii would be a difficult task for them to act like a cold calculating impersonal machine, yet this is what is expected of them.

Carol appeared with the coffee and a few snacks, and the boys followed her in and took up their seats. John had only half heard the news, but he knew it would be on again later on a different channel. John said 'you know…one would think that after thirty years of questions and enquiry, and all this furore debate and contention now emerging, that I would be heartily sick of it all, but my interest is just as strong as it ever was, and I suppose the subject will always torment me until some answers, one way or the other, are forthcoming. I wish to god they would find the missing bones or a divine creator with a host of angels would appear." Thomas interjected. "Or some huge flying saucers appearing like in the film Independence Day, coming to tell us that we are their property."

John laughed, "yes ... even that would be preferable to just not knowing. In any case, after the initial shock, people would gradually accept it all, and anyway they'd have no choice. Any shock is cured in time, that's all it takes, alone with quite a few adjustments of course. It would be preposterous to reach the point of leaving for the stars and still not knowing for sure where we came from."

John had often discussed the perplexities of the past with his sons, who were both interested in unexplained topics. In particular the 'ooparts' or out of place artefacts that disturb the historians, and because of this are confined to some dusty corner of a museum and largely ignored. An ornate silver vase blasted out of quarry rock. Chains of fine gold found in coal seams, as well as a high-quality machined steel cube. Items made of platinum dated from a time long before the period of our accepted ability to process it, with the very high temperatures involved. Aerodynamically feasible model aeroplanes classified as birds. Legends of antediluvian civilisations and people casually recorded in biblical texts as having lived for centuries as humans of the future will no doubt be doing centuries from now.

Ancient Sanskrit writings indicating a knowledge of the atomic structure of matter and of vimanas or flying craft. Ancient knowledge consigned to the flames through ignorance and fear may have taught us so much. Ancient knowledge and advancement may have progressed in a series of peaks and troughs, but what caused the troughs? Although we are currently in an upward mode, the much talked about possibility or asteroidal impact could put us or at least any survivors, straight back into the Stone Age.

When researching his data for the third alternative, John had bagged up any old paperbacks he could get hold of on the UFO's and associated phenomena, and some had written of rather fantastic subjects such as inner earth people and stories of green children emerging from a pit and claiming no sun shone in their world. All clearly set down in chronicles from the Middle Ages by people who did actually exist in those times.

He had read of ancient legends clearly stating humans arrived from outer space. One such ancient Indian legend even specified the area as the Lohit valley. If all those stars that expired in supernovae prior to our own solar system emerging, had at least one planet with intelligent life, they could surely have had enough time to advance to the point of allowing at least some of them to escape the end of their star. Where are all these people? Is space littered with star ships and long dead crews who had never found a suitable world, after generations of floating through the void or is the rather mind-boggling thought that we are the first and entirely alone, really true?

It seems a preposterous consideration given all the molecular groups being detected in space. Conditions are surely in place for a multitude of biological accidents as some people assume was responsible for our own and indeed every other earthly species.

John had read of alien artefacts on the moon and Mars, UFO's entering and leaving the seas. Emanating from the centre of the earth, in and out of a hole in the Polar Regions. No matter how fantastic, someone had presented a case for it. John knew one thing for sure. There were far more questions than there were answers regarding it all.

John snapped out of his reverie with a slight jump as he realised Carol was tapping his arm thinking he had dozed off. She was drawing his attention to the fact that the programme was about to continue and handed him a cup of coffee.

The scene was of the panel of jurists filing back in through the door and taking up their seats. They were seen talking amongst themselves and sifting through various papers. One or two walked to a distinguished looking grey-haired gentleman in the front row, they appeared to be comparing notes and discussing a few points with him. John guessed that he would be the foreman or spokesman for the group.

As the murmuring died away, David Villiers came through the door and took up a position in front of the panel. He began to speak. "Ladies and Gentlemen, have you been able to reach a conclusion or verdict on what seems to be the most logical assumption, according to the evidence presented to you, for how we humans came to be?"

Sure enough, the grey-haired gentleman in the front row gathered up his papers, stood up and prepared to speak.

CHAPTER III

THE VERDICT

"We, as members of this panel, were invited to assess and consider all the factors put to us, in as impartial a manner as possible, concerning the various assumptions people hold, with regard to the monumental question of their origins, or how we humans came to be."

"The first consideration, that of biblical human creation as laid down in the story Genesis, has been accepted as truth by many generations of people over the centuries, and indeed still is. With the coming of the so-called age of enlightenment, and the progress of science, it has become arbitrary and controversial and unacceptable to many, particularly those trained in the cold detached logic of science that has been knocking on the Church's door for many decades, one might almost say for centuries, at least since the time Galileo with his telescope had found that earth is not the centre of all creation."

"Nevertheless, if the story of divine creation has provided comfort and peace of mind and a meaning to life for so many people, then this in itself is sufficient reason to accept it, and in any case who is to stand up and say it did not happen, perhaps in relation to the creation event known as our so-called 'big bang', where science itself struggles to account for the mystical appearance of matter from nothing before it?"

"However, the special story in Genesis of' all creation being completed within seven days *can* only be supported with blind faith, and whereas reasoning and logic are all a feature of the advanced human brain, however we acquired it, blind faith is not.

"Nevertheless, scientific theory and assumption, is itself often being revised, rewritten or disposed of altogether. Most particularly in the science of astrophysics. Many people sense a higher presence than any human is capable of aspiring to, and although the advancement of science threatens their beliefs, the Darwinian argument does not seem strong enough to divert them."

"When we look around us on earth, or deep into the heart of the universe then into the smallest particles of matter, we see evidence of a force. Either the life force of nature or of human creation, or the strange forces at work that hold every particle of matter together, from a galaxy to a garden fork. The more we peer outward into the universal depths, or inward with our electron microscopes, the more we realise how much we don't know."

"We certainly agree with the statement that the universe is not only stranger than we imagine but stranger than we can imagine. We have hardly begun to understand it. How do we explain this colossal explosive event, responsible for the initial beginnings of the universe? How do we quantify this force or perhaps 'creator,' that such creation, evident to our astronomers and astrophysicists obviously implies?"

"Perhaps when the obvious over-endowments of the human brain, with its excess of cellular material provided by some as yet unidentified process or Perhaps donor, become fully utilised, then no questions will remain unanswered."

"The rapid advancement of science is clearly indicated in the consideration, that in a single person's lifetime, a flimsy string bag of an aeroplane took to the air and the process culminated with humans walking on the moon. All achieved within 66 years. It staggers the imagination to contemplate at such a rate of advancement that humans might be capable of if we survive all the celestial threats, after a time period of fifty million years."

"Our so-called cousins and ancestors the apes have already had this amount of evolutionary time since the earliest primates, yet never attempt anything other than their earthly tasks relative to their survival, unless cleverly trained to do things they would not naturally do in all those colonies. Their brains still remain tiny and undeveloped, when they ought to be the dominant earthly species. We have been told, that a natural evolution from simian kind, assumes that apes were indirectly responsible for Newton's laws of the universe, or Einstein's theories, and some would see this as a far more preposterous supposition than accepting a divine creator as the motivating force of all that celestial wonderment."

"It is probable therefore, that greater minds than ours, possessed by future generations will not only answer all the questions so puzzling to us, but will find it difficult to comprehend how things so clear to them, were so hard for us to understand. Yet our mammoth task here, during this simple exercise, was to attempt to quantify this mysterious force or process that produced the precious gift of intelligence that will make all our futuristic achievements possible. Was it a simian bequest? A gift from God? Or perhaps from the gods? A biological accident, never to be repeated?"

"When we consider all the human geniuses and immense creativity and watch from our armchairs Martian scenery unfolding before us from safely landed probes, replaced in the not too distant future by human boot prints, it does indeed seem incredible that the most scientifically acceptable theory for the human brain is a simian bequest above all else, when they have achieved so little for themselves with all that immense evolution."

"This amazing human brain, made up of brain cells equal in number to every star in the galaxy, cries out for a more logical and acceptable explanation. Yet for all its capabilities, it has a darker negative side that makes the human species, with the possible exception of the cat, the only creature that kills for pleasure, therefore humans can plumb the depths of depravity as well as aspiring to the currently impossible."

"Could a divine infallible creator produce such an obvious contrast in mental ability? If we accept the Church's teachings, that this is so, and moreover it was purposely done, then this implies that such a creator would be responsible for every heinous crime and unspeakable act on earth today."

"We of the panel have learned much ourselves in comparison with our previous assumptions. It was clear that 160 years ago the advancement of science even then, was crying out for an alternative to beliefs only sustainable with blind faith. Consequently, Charles Darwin's theory was their god substitute, but his breath-taking assumption was no more breath-taking than a certain Bishop Usher stating that creation occurred in 4004 BC around breakfast time."

"A.R. Wallace sought some unknown variable or exterior force to explain the advanced human intellect. Today, 160 years later we still search for the vital fossils necessary to prove it all, and no natural history museum anywhere in the world can produce the fossils of all the transitional species necessary, on the long road from primordial lungfish leaving the ancient seas, and finally standing upright as humans."

"We are held firmly in our species, each unto their kind, by our genetic code or chromosomes, preventing the chaos that would result in any cross-species mating. How were these factors overcome, to allow all those changes of species, the evidence for which still eludes us?"

"Even science fails to rescue a natural evolution from the primates with the studies of human blood showing no, connection with the ancient apes and bipeds, and the results of mitochondrial DNA analysis indicating a recent origin for humankind. Where then, did the already evolved Cro-Magnon people come from? No-one has the answer."

"Although many obvious questions need to be answered regarding the Darwinian viewpoint, questions also require to be addressed, regarding the beliefs of biblical creation. As said, a divine infallible almighty creator would surely have much to answer for in the more negative and heinous capabilities of the human. These factors then, would appear to indicate a more fallible creator or creators."

"The obvious threats in celestial debris and things occurring in deep space, with colliding galaxies and so forth, would also seem to indicate things are less than perfect in the universal creation also. These then, are our comments with regard to the primary and most contentious views held by the so-called creationists and evolutionists."

"We were also asked to consider a so-called ' third alternative, we are aware that this is not the author's own special theory, but has been in place for decades, one could almost say generations, since the late Charles Fort, postulated that humankind might be property!"

"This theory has a substantial amount of circumstantial evidence in its favour, but circumstantial evidence is not factual evidence, and as far as is known in spite of any claims by the ufologists to the contrary, we do not possess so much as a shirt button from a visiting extra-terrestrial, or a single artefact brought back from the many claims of alien abduction by the victims or abductees."

"Of course, it could be logically argued, that the abductors, who not only traverse interstellar space, also allegedly enhanced, or at least their predecessors enhanced, our mental development, would be unlikely to be so careless with their shirt buttons or allow abductees to sneak off with an alien navigational aid or sextant and so we do not seem to possess a single artefact that could be claimed to be not of this earth. Nevertheless, for all we know, the ufologists could be perfectly correct in their allegations of a cover up, as it has been shown with all those released documents deletions and retentions that with regard to written reports there is a cover up and in information that aliens somehow created us would certainly be a first-class item for a cover up in view of what the release of such data would cause."

"And so, only the circumstantial evidence has been presented to us for consideration. Together with other data, we have been made aware of the existence of a branch of science called exobiology, and the people qualified in it are termed exobiologists, which is said to mean an expert in alien life forms."

"If we have no alien life-forms as authorities bodies continually state, where then did they get their training in order to become exobiologists? It would be a science without a subject. Or are we to assume that they have had access to recovered alien entities? They postulate that alien life-forms would not be like us at all."

"Microbiologists will argue that the process of photosynthesis is widely divergent and also, there is great variation in plant life and in the living creatures on earth, and so anyone's guess will do, with regard to what we would expect to find on another life supporting world. However, an analysis of such flora growing on another world with air and water would no doubt reveal a cellular structure, DNA of sorts and an evolution from basic amino acids, just as happened on earth. Everything everywhere will be made of atoms. The universe is predominantly hydrogen and the list of elements will probably be quite short and obviously finite." "Multi-cellular reproducing creatures elsewhere will almost certainly have much in common with us, and the life process or force may be universal in some respects. Humans appear to be the evolutionary ideal as creative beings, and the life force may produce a similar body form elsewhere."

"We find it preposterous to consider that humans could be the only intelligent life form, when told that there are more stars than there are grains of sand on every earthly beach. And would find it equally preposterous to accept that they would be all less advanced than ourselves."

"Therefore, the logical conclusion is, that creatures could exist, who have mastered interstellar travel, and if so, would be well versed in all the sciences, particularly mathematics. They may have catalogued, studied and manipulated the DNA of many other fauna and flora and their evolutionary history. Learned people have postulated that earth could have been visited in the past by such beings and that it manifests itself in certain artwork and earthly legends and rock paintings, where the ancients appeared to be struggling to depict what they had seen."

"Interestingly and no doubt coincidentally, the Darwinian theory for human appearance, biblical creation, and the third alternative have certain factors in common. We could discover buried artefacts that were indisputably alien to this earth, and we could equally discover buried fossil links to vindicate Darwin. Also, both the third alternative and biblical creation could involve a form of second coming. Biblical writings specifying this, already exist and with regard to an alien creation thesis, there would also surely have to be a point when such creators would feel we were ready for such revelations in a form of alien second coming, particularly as our negative aggressive and faulty genes retard our progress toward true civilisation enormously and such hypothetical alien creators of yore could, if capable of such clever manipulation up to 100 thousand years ago, surely cure our negative and undesirable traits practically at a stroke today."

"And so, after all the words, conjecture and postulation our verdict is, that there can be no verdict, and that it is currently impossible for our limited mental processes, knowledge and discovery, to produce one. And for all we know, the force or unknown variable that we so dismally fail to quantify, may not yet wish us to do so. And before we borrow the statement of our eminent anthropologist when referring to the Darwinian concept, we would emphasise that his statement equally applies to any theory we could put forward for how we humans came to be. No-one can stand up and declare 'this is how it was."

"However, perhaps we should add, that when we say no-one, we mean of course no-one on earth, for all we know, the truth could very well be...out there. And that is the end of our statement."

When the spokesman sat down and began shuffling his papers together, John and his family and of course the millions of viewers the programme attracted, noticed a very strange thing, perhaps unprecedented on television. When David Villiers appeared, (the programme's producer) they started to clap in reaction to the spokesman's address, technicians, sound engineers and all the various studio staff seemed to appear and filled the gap between the entrance door and the front bench where the panel had now risen. And they began slowly filing out, row by row through the door as the staff parted, still clapping until each of them had passed through the door. The staff then fell silent and melted away. Only David Villiers remained and began to speak.

"Well...there you have it. After all the words and evidence, no verdict. But how would you have dealt with it? What would your verdict have been? I'm quite sure that this type of enquiring programme will not be the last to deal with this contentious issue, and the enquiry will continue for quite some time to come. May I ask that you do not send any reactionary letters to this studio regarding this programme. We have had a deluge of mail to deal with from the pre-programme advertisements alone. Most of which has been redirected either to the publishers or the author of the book upon which the programme was based."

"Anyone who may write in with appreciative comments on the quality of the programme for example, then for this we thank you. Our efforts will now be directed into the subject of the next programme to follow this one. And we therefore have little time to deal with correspondence. Now it only remains for me to say, on behalf of everyone responsible for the programme, thank you and goodnight."

John and his family sat quietly for a while, either stretching their legs or just looking at the television screen. Finally, Carol said, "It was so interesting that I can't believe we've been sitting here for an hour and a half, it doesn't seem that long, docs it?" "It certainly doesn't." John replied. "David presented it very well. I had a feeling that they would come out with a verdict that according to the evidence, the third alternative seems to be the most compelling conclusion, particularly after David listed all the factors. I'm glad they didn't really. Not because I don't want it to have happened particularly, but because I've spent so long on my soapbox saying no-one has all the answers, and the subject remains pretty much a mystery."

"Anyway, I'll bet the phones and fax machines are buzzing already. The scholars and academics will all be itching to get their views and comments into the next programme. It won't be the 'How did it happen' series, I understand it will be called simply 'Origins'. I don't envy the anchorman; they'll all want to talk at once. I don't want any part of it. I'll obviously retain my interest, but I've said all I want to say on any radio or TV programme"

"I can just imagine some of the comments. Particularly with regard to the third alternative. Rubbish, preposterous, sheer science fiction. They won't even consider any circumstantial evidence"

Carol replied, "oh well…we'll have to wait and see I suppose, I know one thing, I can feel one of my 'heads' coming on, I should have worn my glasses. I'm only used to my half hour soaps and sit-coms. I'm going to take a pill and turn in. See you later; try not to put the main light on when you come in. I'll leave your bedside on." "OK darling" John replied, "see you later." As Carol disappeared, John turned to the boys and reminded them to finish their projects for College tomorrow. They exchanged goodnights as John went into his study for his nightcap.

CHAPTER IV

THE AFTERMATH

The day after the programme went out, John felt that his previous fears were groundless as to whether he would feel like stepping out of the door or hiding himself away. David Villiers had handled the programme so well, he felt an unbiased and pretty fair presentation had been achieved, and as this was what John had tried to portray in his book, he was quite satisfied.

He had certainly achieved his major aim in getting people interested and talking about the topic, and successfully dispelled the notion that it was safe to assume that any theory for origins was sacrosanct and unassailable. As no illuminating conclusion had been reached, the debates would no doubt rumble on for decades to come. But now there would be more than just two groups at the table.

John therefore was quite satisfied that he had made his point, but the interest and debate that he had generated, should in his opinion, have been occurring long beforehand. Many people who had not looked into the problems and shortcomings themselves, on what he still regarded as the most likely theory for origins, namely the theory subscribed to by his own profession, were quietly led to assume that all was well.

It reminded John of a cynical remark he had encountered when researching UFO magazines to write the third alternative. An item commenting on the Roswell incident had said "Why bother about the facts if it makes an interesting story." People who are not inordinately religious and leant toward the Darwinian hypothesis, simply put their trust in science. And the scientists connected with John's own profession had, in his opinion, to some extent, let them down.

Apart from a few exceptions, which were the more honest and open-minded members of the field of anthropological studies, who had stated the facts regarding the paucity of fossil evidence to support the Darwinian theory, the majority, for the most part had knowingly or perhaps unknowingly lulled the average layman into a false sense of security regarding the validity of the theory, and allowed them to assume it was all settled and unassailable.

There were far more remarks regarding ancestors and cousins than there were references to the unanswered questions with which the theory abounds. No remarks in any public debates ever dealt with the lack of vital links or any perplexity as to why they continually seem to elude us, when other animal bones are apparent in such abundance from so long ago. Now, he felt that this situation had been adequately addressed.

The next day, John ran the boys to school then bought copies of the primary newspapers. Of the four that he bought, three of them ran a lengthy feature on the programme dealing with his book. One of them had it as part of the front page, under a prominent headline that read 'Monkey Trial 2000.'

Before the remarks about the programme, there was a lead-in concerning the famous American lawyer Clarence Darrow, who rigorously defended John Scopes in 1925 for teaching Darwinian evolution in his Tennessee school, and found himself in jail. Partly for his own safety, as the outraged townsfolk wanted to lynch him. They had strong religious views and were therefore quite opposed to the godless Darwinian theory, that took a biblical creator out of the picture altogether and opposed their rather comforting beliefs.

John felt that in one sense they were rather like the senior Church elders who refused to look through Galileo's telescope, in fear of having their entrenched views undermined. Strangely, he also quite realised that today it is the turn of the so-called evolutionists to go on the defensive and resist any challenge or alternative suggestions for the appearance of humankind.

The Church had obviously bent with the wind over the last few generations, and generous concessions had been made to science. Even the Vatican now has special religious policy meetings and discussions on how to adjust to the situation if extra-terrestrials reveal themselves in a discovered signal, or otherwise make themselves known to us.

In spite of any concessions by the Church, people's individual beliefs in their various creeds were just as strong as ever in some cases. The Christian teachings in the New Testament are admirable doctrines, and John felt that to preach love and forgiveness was surely a better policy than putting a contract out on anyone saying a wrong word against it and encouraging murder in its name.

His assessment of the newspaper reports was that they were positive and encouraging and highlighted the previous lack of discussion and strong assumptions in place of hard fossil evidence. But John was quite aware, that they would also gleefully report the disparaging remarks he felt sure were to come, when all the experts, scholars and academics get their chance on the follow-up programme, to dismiss any challenges they felt were appearing against their sacrosanct theories.

After John had analysed all the newspaper reports, he was soon back at his word processor finishing off another manuscript from his mass of scribbled notes. He never experienced time passing as quickly as it seemed to do when he was at his P.C. Soon it was time to pick the boys up from college, which was about half a mile outside the town.

John gave in to pressure and agreed to a meal in a fast food outlet in the town. He knew that his wife Carol would just pop something in the microwave when she got in, which was usually just before they got home. Saturday and Sunday seemed to be the only time lately, that they all sat down to a cooked meal, and sometimes not even then. With so many 'two for the price of one' pub meals on offer these days, it seemed an easier option than buying big joints of meat and all the preparation and dishwashing that went with it, when for around £20 they could all eat out. They were becoming a 'why bother' family. A trend John never really felt comfortable about.

It was a cold January evening with a frost already starting to form, but the meal had warmed them all up a little. Carol was a secretary in a local school and always got home early. After garaging the car, they all filed through the rear door rubbing their hands. John noticed the kitchen was not as warm as it usually was and asked, "Anything wrong with the heating?" John immediately knew something was wrong, not only because of the crunching noises their feet were making on the kitchen vynl, but because of his wife's body language, which spelt stress. She was puffing heavily on a cigarette, as she sat stiffly on a stool and her usual cheerful greeting had not come.

"What's wrong darling?" he enquired. "Take a look at that," she said, nodding toward the 10" wide glass window that ran vertically beside the door. "And that," she said, glancing at a smooth stone on the breakfast bar, like those on a beach. Alongside the stone were half a dozen elastic bands and a smoothed-out piece of A4 paper covered in red crayoned crucifix type crosses. It contained no remarks or message, just the mass of crosses. John glanced back at the hole a moment, then said, "are you alright? It didn't hit you did it?" "Oh no," she replied, "I found it when I came in. Do you think someone has been watching the house? They must have known no-one was in"…"Not necessarily," John replied. "These dark evenings they can do this anytime and get away without being identified." John tried to comfort and reassure Carol. "It's probably just an isolated incident, some religious nut. It will only be a 'one-off' incident I'm sure."

Carol looked unconvinced. "Look here now…one missile doesn't make a war" he said grinning, "I'm not going to going to be able to sleep much tonight, I know it," she said apprehensively. "Don't worry about it, I'll stay up late and catch up on some work and sleep in tomorrow, if you'll run the boys to school."

His sons had not spoken at all but just looked at their mother. Now they both put their arms around her and then guided her into the living room. "I'll clean up this lot and put a piece of plywood in the window frame until tomorrow, then I'll replace it."

He picked up the paper smothered in crosses by the corner with his finger and thumb and wondered if there was any point in bothering the police. If it got into the evening paper it might spark off another copycat offence. He felt sure that whoever did it, more than likely took the necessary precautions against leaving fingerprints and even if they did, John couldn't imagine the police fingerprinting the entire town over a broken window, and Carol's prints may be on it. Nevertheless, if the perpetrator was stupid enough to do such a juvenile thing, perhaps they hadn't bothered about prints and the perpetrator may well be known to the police, and their prints may be on file.

John decided to put the items in a polythene bag and hand them in to the local police station in the morning. John tried to think which part of his book had angered the perpetrator so much. He had felt a little anxious when writing the work and dissecting and analysing biblical texts and questioning religious beliefs, but he had put his anxiety down to his former Catholic upbringing. The questions he asked may have appeared cold and detached to an extremely religious person, but he could not at the time of writing it, find any other softer approach in asking them.

Who would the next stone be from? He wondered, the Animal Rights extremists? He had already received many abusive letters from them. Again, his attention to the lack of intellect in apes was not a derogatory assessment of them, it was just a fact. He had merely wished to highlight the enormous gulf between them and humans and their qualifications to be deemed ancestors, that naturally became humans.

That evening, John found himself continually trying to change the subject, but the conversation always drifted back to the act of vandalism and any possible future occurrences, right up to when the boys went to bed.

John had broached the subject of moving closer to the city centre than their present suburban location and pointed out the advantages he saw in such a move. Once the boys had been assured they would not be uprooted from college, they both seemed alright about it. But Carol was worried about losing touch with her circle of friends and seemed convinced she *would* lose touch with them.

During their evening's discussion, which had taken a stone through their window to promote, instead of staring at the TV, and someone hushing another when trying to converse, the TV had not been switched on at all. Certain things the boys had obviously been bottling up, all came out and John realised more than ever, that the publicity of his book and now the television programme and the combined effects, were now reaching out to his own family.

Although the events the boys spoke of seemed trivial to John, he could see that they were not so unimportant to them, by the tone of their voices and their obvious disgust when telling their stories. Thomas had said, "Do you know what one little sprog said to me? "Hey, your Dad's the monkey man, isn't he? Good job he rode off so quickly on his bike, or I would have clouted the little sod." Robert recounted some of the childish comments he had endured. The monkey like noises behind his back and the notes of the X-Files theme continually being whistled near him.

John had tried to reassure them by saying he had expected it and that it would soon die down, but as soon as he said it he realised just how long his nickname 'Tommo' had lasted. It had gone on so long that eventually people thought that it really was his name.

The next day John handed in his strange bag of items to a bemused desk officer at the local police station. After a short interview he left, assured that they would be in touch if there were any developments. He was advised to leave a light on when the house was empty at night, at least for a week or two.

His family quickly regained their spirits and seemed to have put the incident behind them and spent the weekends driving closer to the city and looking at properties.

Then came the second incident. One morning John awoke with a start as he heard the piercing scream and the shattering of what sounded like a bottle of liquid dropping. He ran downstairs, and his wife Carol was standing at the door holding her hands to her mouth. There was a pool of milk on the doorstep with pieces of broken bottle in it, and Carol's legs were splashed with milk droplets. Swinging grotesquely, with its arms in the air, was a soft toy monkey someone had tied to the outside light with string. It slowly turned as though displaying its charms in a slow twirl.

John was the first to laugh, and then the boys who had followed him downstairs having also been woken by their Mother's scream and the breaking bottle. When John had cut it down and consigned it to the dustbin where it looked as though it had come from in the first place, he returned to find Carol again stiffly perched on her stool puffing heavily on a cigarette. She did it every time she was concerned or wound up about something. John searched for comforting words that had already been said by the boys who had been working on her before he came in.

"Don't worry yourself over this, we'll soon be out of here. Anyway, there hasn't been anything really serious has there?" After a few seconds Carol said, rather frostily, "I don't suppose you've heard anything from the police about the stone thrower?" "No...as a matter of fact I haven't." He replied. After a final desperate attempt at defusing the situation, John sensed success when he noticed a flicker of a smile as he described the scene confronting the milkman, John said, "It's a wonder he didn't drop the bottle."

A few months passed before the tension eased, Carol had been jumpy about every little noise, that normally would not have bothered her. Then, they found themselves loading all their possessions into a large furniture van. John had warned the boys that their mother was still touchy and rather upset about leaving and to be careful what they said. They would all miss the house for a while.

As John had suspected, their routine in their new home slowly began to become established, and they all began to appreciate the larger space now available, particularly the boys, with all the sound equipment and guitars, as they both played in local pop groups, and especially their personal computers. John noticed Carol's behaviour patterns slowly returning to normal. Their new home was fairly near to John's friend David Villiers and his wife, who joined them in polishing off a few bottles of champagne in a memorable housewarming party, with a room to spare, the Villiers' were their overnight guests.

David had revealed that the ratings of the programme 'How did it happen' had been immense, and so they looked on it as a double celebration. A rival channel was trying to tempt David Villiers over to them with attractive salary offers. David had manfully resisted but had admitted to John after a few glasses of champagne that he didn't see himself as an exception to the rule with regard to the old adage 'everyone has his price'.

A programme, largely put out to redress the balance as it were, had recently been shown and also hosted by David. It reminded John of the Question Time format and was made up of academics, scholars, theologians and astrophysicists. And as John had expected, they took a firm no nonsense line and stuck rigidly to their established ideals and had no time, except for one or two exceptions, for anything radical or controversial. John and his family had watched the programme, but it failed to produce the same impact or effect they had experienced with 'How did it happen?'

John refused to appear on any more TV or radio shows. It was clear the established order as it were, still seemed determined to bring the heretic to book, but John had been equally determined they would not, and had grown rather tired of continually explaining his reasons why he would not appear, which was that, in the first place he had nothing to defend, and that any radical suggestions and theories that had emerged in *The Human Enigma* and subsequently on the TV programme had been the work of others and John had produced them as alternative belief systems that had some circumstantial evidence to support them.

And so finally, his adversaries in their frustration at not being able to corner their quarry, gave up the chase, except for one or two that continued to snipe away at him in the media at every opportunity.

At breakfast after their champagne party, with everyone decidedly more subdued than they had been the night before, John was sorting through his mail; one letter was from his literary agent and was outlining the terms of a contact for a film company which was interested in the potential of his latest book, *Pillars of Fire*.

As time went by, life never seemed so good for John and his family. There were no more unpleasant events and they began to do things together more. John and David agreed that the film contract was a good excuse for another party, this time at David's house and as David collected vintage wines and had a pretty good cellar, it should be a memorable evening. At the weekend John and Carol decided on a trip to the local zoo, something they had not done for some time. Surprisingly, to both of them, the boys expressed a wish to join them.

It was a fine spring day as they slowly walked past the chimpanzee enclosure. John was deep in the study of a map showing the layout of the zoo. Suddenly with a plopping noise a rather substantial portion of sloppy mud struck John in the face and fell onto the map, making it quite unreadable. They all stopped and fell silent. With one smooth movement John used three fingers to scrape the mud from his face and flicked it onto the ground. He looked at Carol and the boys whose mouths seemed strangely contorted. He looked at the chimpanzee who was the obvious perpetrator of this outrage, and it had its lips curled back as though laughing at him to add insult to injury.

Thomas broke the silence and said, "well Dad...it looks as though they've got their own back on you at last." At that they all exploded with laughter except John. He wiped the remaining mud away with his handkerchief, but his serious look only made his family laugh the harder. They were hooting with laughter as John finally succumbed and threw his head back and roared with laughter. The four of them hardly noticed the curious glances they were getting as they walked toward the exit still bellowing with laughter.

***